THE SEVEN YEAR JOURNEY TO HOPE

Ken Morrison

Tellwell Talent

www.tellwell.ca

ISBN

978-1-77370-591-0 (Hardcover)

978-1-77370-593-4 (Paperback)

978-1-77370-592-7 (eBook)

I dedicate this book to my wife
Gloria who believed in me.

Table of Contents

Prologue

I WAS BORN IN 1828 ON A PIG FARM JUST OUT SIDE A TOWN called HEBRON ILLINOISE a two day run by wagon to CHICAGO.

My first memory of the farm is that of being chased by a big pig and seeing my father laughing at me. I learned very young to run fast and hide. My father would go to town several times a week to get pig feed and food scraps in wooden barrels. I would help him cook them in an iron pot on an open fire outside the barn. When the food was ready I would carry it in a pail and dump it in a wooden trough in the pig pen. as fast as I could carry it the pigs would fight over it until the food was all gone. We would do this every day. One day I dropped a pail of hot food on the ground, and my father yelled at me and went for his walking stick. I knew I was going to get a beating, and so I ran around the barn with my father chasing me. I panicked and blindly ran into my father, who had stopped running and was waiting for me. He laughed at me and gave me a severe beating. I remember my mother washing the blood off my face and telling me to be more careful with the pig feed. I can't remember my parents ever showing me any real kindness. My father would hit me with his walking stick for the smallest thing I did wrong. I could not understand why.

When I turned ten years old my father told me I had to sleep in the barn, and so I cleared a space in the corner of the hayloft to sleep in. When it got cold I would pull hay over myself to keep warm. When it was not so bad my father would put me on a big pig's back and tell me to hang on to its ear, and then he would kick the pig so that it would run around the barn yard, and I would have to hang on for dear life. One time I fell off, and the pig stepped on my leg, cutting it open. My father laughed at this. My mother cleaned the blood off my leg and wrapped a cloth around it and told me to be more careful around the pigs. One day, the biggest pig was chasing me, and so I got a shovel and hit him on his testicles. He screamed and tore around the barn. He did not chase me anymore, but I knew he would bite me if he got the chance, and so I kept a close eye on him.

Sometimes my parents gave me nothing to eat, and so I would sneak into the hen house at night and take some eggs and eat them raw. By the time I turned twelve I was being treated like a slave and was being beaten almost every day. And so I made a plan to run away, not a very good plan, but it worked, and I am here to tell you about it.

Chapter 1

The Beginning

MY STORY STARTED YESTERDAY—MAY 12ᵀᴴ, 1840—MY 12th birthday. That morning I heard loud voices coming from the house,so I went up to the back door to see what was going on. My grandfather had died two months ago of the fever, and his lawyer had come to read his last will and testament. He made my parents very angry. My father chased the lawyer out of the house. Off he drove in his buggy. My mother yelled at my father, saying that my grandfather had left the farm to me.

"This farm is mine," my father said, "and no snot-nosed little bugger is going to take it away from me!"

"He does own the farm," my mother screamed at him. "And when he turns twenty-one he can throw us off the farm if he wants to!"

My father grabbed the kitchen table and flipped it over and stomped around the room, saying it was his farm, and that he had worked like a slave for it, and no little bastard was going to put him off it. Then he said he should not have married my mother, because he was not even my real father. My mother said it would be a shame if something bad were to happen to me and I died. My father said: "Yes, we will kill him." And then he laughed so loud it frightened me, and I started to shake all over, so I ran to the barn and hid in the hayloft.

When I turned ten my father started to treat me like a slave and made me sleep in the barn, so the hayloft became my safe place. The morning after the lawyer's visit, my father came to the barn. I could see he was angry with me. He grabbed me by the shirtfront and slammed me up against the barn wall and slapped me across my face. I started to cry, so he slapped me again, and I slipped to the floor. He pulled to my feet and told me I had better get all my chores done or I would get a good beating and no supper, then he left and walked back to the house.

I could not believe what had just happened, so I worked very hard all morning. After putting hay down for our two milk cows I felt very tired. I sat down in the hay to have a rest and fell asleep. When I did not bring the morning milk to the house my mother came looking for me and found me asleep in the hay. She kicked me in the ribs and slapped my face. I woke with a start. Then my mother grabbed me by my hair and dragged me to the house. She told my father that she had found me sleeping in the barn and that I should get a good beating for it. My father picked up his walking stick and beat me all over my body. The pain was so terrible that I don`t remember when he stopped hitting me. After the beating he told me to go back to the barn and finish my chores. I could not get up from the floor, so he kicked me and pulled me to my feet and pushed me out the back door. I stumbled back to the barn. When I got inside I thought to myself that, of all the beatings I had gotten, this one was the worse. I cried for a long time, but the pain did not go away. That night I went to our hen house and found four eggs and ate them raw. I had been eating raw eggs for a long time, because they were not giving me much to eat.

That night I decided to run away. I barely slept because of the pain and because I was so intent on making plans to run away. I got up before sun-up and walked down our lane and started to run towards Herbron, the nearest town. I ran for the whole day, but I did not find it. I must of missed it in my haste to get away from my parents. That night I slept under some bushes by the side of the road. The pain was bad, but the further I got away from my parents the better I felt. The next morning I was awakened by a noise. I looked out of my hiding place to see a wagon coming along the road. I was terrified that it was my father out looking for me. When the wagon got close I saw that it was an old man with a load of vegetables, so I stepped out of my hiding place and waved to him. He stopped his wagon and asked me where I was going. I did not know, so I pointed in the same direction he was going and asked him for a ride. He looked at me for a minute, and then he told me he was going to Chicago and would be pleased for the company. I got up on the wagon and sat beside him. He asked me my name.

"Kaleb," I said. "My name is Kaleb Jakobs

The old man looked at me for a moment then said i could call him Albert and smiled at me. I said i was pleased to meet him."

,. At that he patted me on my head. After a while the rocking of the wagon made me tired and I started to nod off. Albert asked me if I were tired, and I told him I was. so he got an old coat from under his seat and wrapped it around me and pulled me close to him and I fell asleep.

When I woke up the wagon had stopped and was off to the side of the road and Albert was cooking something over a small fire. It smelled good, so I got down from the wagon and walked over to the fire. Albert looked up. "You, hungry?"

I told him I was, and he gave me a tin plate with some eggs and fried bread on it. I sat down on a large rock and ate the food, and then he gave me a tin mug of hot, sweet tea. It made me feel a lot better. When I was finished, Albert asked me if I was going all the way to Chicago with him.

"I'd sure like to," I mumbled. "If you don't mind, that is."

He told me I would have to help him, and I told him I would, so he gave me a pail and showed me where the water was. I was to water his two horses. It took two pails each to satisfy their thirst. When we started down the road, Albert asked me if I knew how to drive a team of horses. I told him I did, so he handed the reins to me so he could have a short nap. I was so happy to be able to help. That afternoon it got quite warm and I took Albert's coat off. He looked at me for a few minutes, and then asked me about the stains on my shirt and pants. I just looked down and said nothing. When we stopped for an afternoon break he asked me to take off my shirt so he could take a look. He touched my back and I flinched and he said: "Oh, my God, what happened to you?"

so I told him what my parents had done to me. He looked shocked and asked why, and I told him about our farm and how my grandfather left the farm to me and how I would be able to take ownership of the farm when I turned twenty-one. I told him about hearing my parents say that they would kill me before I could get the farm, and so I ran away. Albert told me he could help me. He asked me to take off my pants and he cleaned my wounds and put on some liniment he had for his horses. I told him it hurt real bad. He said it would feel better soon, and it did.

That evening we stopped at a farm Albert visited each time he went to Chicago. He told me he would take some of their vegetables to market in payment for sleeping over. While we were eating supper, Albert asked the lady if she still had any clothes left by her grown-up sons. She said she would look in the attic. After supper I was sitting on the porch while Albert looked after his horses when the lady came out of the house with a box and put it down in front of me. She said that some of the clothes might be all right for me, so I opened the box and took out a shirt and looked at it. The lady asked me to try it on, so I took Albert's coat off and the lady looked at my wounds. She told me Albert had told her my story and she helped me put on the shirt. It was too big, so she turned up the sleeves to fit. Then I took off my pants. The lady started to cry as she helped me put on a pair of pants. Then I took out a pair of almost new, but scuffed boots that almost fit me. I knew I would grow into them soon, and so for now I laced them up tight so that I could walk in them just fine.

Albert and I slept in the hayloft. In the morning we had a breakfast like I had never had before. There was bacon, eggs, fried potatoes, toasted bread, milk, and hot sweet tea. When we were ready to leave I thanked the lady for the clothes she had given me. She gave me a big hug and kissed me on the cheek and said she was glad to help. I got up on the wagon seat and thought my heart would burst with pride as I looked at my first pair of almost-new boots. That afternoon we came to Albert's first stop, a large store on the outskirts of Chicago. I helped Albert unload half of his load and carry it into a back room. When we were finished the store owner gave us some hot food and a hot drink he called coffee. It was sweet and very good. The store owner asked me how long I had been working for Albert.

"Albert's just giving me a ride to Chicago," I said, and looked into my coffee.

"Whatever you gonna do in Chicago?"

"I dunno. I'm coming from a bad place, I guess you could say. I don't know where I'm going next."

"Well, why don't you work with me here in the store."

"What would I be doing?" I asked and looked around.

"Well, clean the store and fill the shelves and help customers find what they're looking for and for that I'll pay you a dollar a week and room and board."

"What's room and board?"

He laughed and said it was a warm bed and all the food I could eat.

I looked at Albert for help and he smiled at me and told me to take the job, and so I told the store owner I would. When Albert was ready to leave I shook his hand and thanked him for his kindness. He gave me a big hug and told me it was a pleasure meeting me and hoped to see me on his next trip to Chicago.

Chapter 2

Chicago

THE STORE OWNER ASKED ME MY NAME AND HE TOLD ME to call him Mr. Ned. Then he showed me a small room in the back of the store and said I could spend the rest of the day fixing it up. As he left he said supper was at six o'clock and breakfast was at six in the morning. I found wooden shipping boxes in the alley outside the store and made some cupboards for my clothes. Mr. Ned brought me some blankets and a pillow for the small iron bed that was in the corner. That was the best night's sleep I had ever had. At breakfast the next morning Mr. Ned introduced me to his wife Martha and their daughter Anne. Then he asked me what I meant when I said I had come from a very bad place. I sighed and told them about my life on the farm and about the beatings I had gotten, and how I had heard my parents say they were going to kill me and how I ran away. "And here I am," I finished.

Mr. Ned had told Martha about my wounds, and so after breakfast Martha asked me to stay so she could see then for herself. i took my shirt off and stood there. Martha looked at my back and started to cry and said" oh, you poor boy what have they done to you. Then she asked me to take off my pants and with a shocked look on her face, examined my leg wounds. she got some hot water and soap and cleaned all my wounds then wrapped them with a clean cloth. my wounds did not hurt much now. Martha cleaned them every day until the scabs started to fall off.

Martha was kind to me and treated me like a son and I grew to love her like a mother. And that was the first day of a two-year adventure with them. I worked hard for Mr. Ned. I liked the store very much and I met lots of nice people. Most of them treated me good. Martha would bring me little treats in the afternoons and I loved playing hide-and-seek with little Anne, and how she would laugh and jump up and down and clap her hands and how Mr. Ned would smile at us.

One night after I had been there for six months, I was putting out the garbage when I spotted someone looking through our garbage and went to see what was going on. When I got close, I saw it was a girl. I asked her what she was doing. She looked up startled to see me standing there. She told me she was looking for something to eat. I could see she was hungry . Her clothes were dirty, and she smelt very bad. I asked her where she lived. She told me her mother had died and her stepfather had tried to touch her, and she did not like it. And so she ran away. I did not know what she meant, but I thought it must be something like the beatings I got. My heart went out to her. I told her that I lived in the store and that she could stay there at night but would have to leave in the morning before Mr. Ned got up. She looked at me for a minute, and then said it would be all right. I asked her her name and she said it was Sam, short for Samantha and she was twelve years old. I told her my name and said I was twelve and going on thirteen . I took her into the store and showed her my room, and said I could make her a bed in the corner of the room. Then I went into the store and got some bread and cold cuts and made her a sandwich and gave her a small bottle of milk. While she was eating, I made her a bed, and then I got our wash tub and half filled it with water and got a bar of soap from the store and laid out a clean shirt and pair of pants and asked her to take a bath and put on the clean clothes. She looked at me with a frown, so I told her she smelled like the garbage I had found her in. At that she took off her clothes and got in the tub, and I took her old clothes and put them in the garbage. when she was finished with her bath, I loaned her my comb to do her hair. With clean clothes and her hair combed, she looked quite nice for a 12-year-old girl. She was the first girl I had known, and I liked her.

The next morning I told Mr. Ned about Sam and what she had told me, and I asked if she could stay with us. He told me he would talk to her and that I should go and find her and bring her to the store. I went looking for Sam and found her sitting on a shipping box next door. I told her Mr. Ned would like to talk to her. She looked at me, and said, "All right?" She smiled, so I took her to see Mr. Ned. Martha was with him. They smiled at her and asked her to sit down. The first thing they asked her was her name and whether she had she gone to school. She told them her name was Samantha Reed and she was twelve years old and that she could read and write a bit, but that she had not liked school much. Martha said they could use help looking after the upstairs and help with little Anne. Martha told her they would pay her a dollar a week and room and board and that she could sleep upstairs. Sam smiled at Martha and said that would be Okay.

○────○○○────○

So Sam went to work that day and liked the work. Sam and I would take turns playing with little Anne. After a short time Sam and I became best of friends. On our day off we would go exploring the south side of Chicago. There were lots of shops, and we found a puppet show we liked. It only cost us a penny each to see it. One day when we were exploring a new area of the south side, Sam slipped her hand into mine. From that day on we would hold hands where ever we went. One afternoon after we had just seen a new puppet show, I gave Sam a big hug and kissed her on her cheek. She pulled away and looked at me, and then kissed me on my lips We were two thirteen year olds experiencing puppy love. Six months later I turned fourteen and Mr. Ned and Martha threw a small birthday supper for me. After supper Martha gave me a gift wrapped in brown paper. When I opened it, I found a silver pocket knife. I took it in my hand and started to cry. It was the first gift anyone had ever given me. Mr. Ned put his arm around me "Happy Birthday, young Kaleb," he said.

○────○○○────○

One day a women asked Mr. Ned if she could get some help with her bags, and so Mr. Ned came and found me working in the back and told me to carry Mrs. Roman's bags for her.

On theway to her house she asked me how long I had worked at the store. I told her two years. Then she asked me if I liked it. I told her Mr. Ned had been good to me. She asked me how old I was. I told her I was fourteen. When we got to her house I put the bags in the kitchen. As I walked through the house I noticed it was a mess and needed a good cleaning. When she came into the kitchen I asked her if she had a house keeper. She said her housekeeper had died and that she could not find a new one. Then she looked at me and asked if I could do housework. I told her I could. She looked at me for a moment, and then asked me if I would like to come and work for her. I asked her what I would have to do. She said I would have to clean the house and run errands for her and she would pay me seven dollars a month and room and board. I told her I would let her know. On the way back to the store I thought about the job offer. I wanted to take it, and so when I got back to the store I told Mr. Ned about the job Mrs. Roman had offered me and asked him what I should do. He told me it was a good job, and that I should take it. He told me he would miss me and that I would be hard to replace.

——oOo——

That night I told Sam that I was leaving to start a new job. She started cry. I told her I would come to see her on my day off and she stopped crying. At the end of the week I said goodbye to everyone and told them I would come back to see them when I could.

——oOo——

When I knocked on Mrs. Romans front door she opened it and smiled at me and told me to come in. She showed me a room off the kitchen that had a real bed and red carpet on the floor. She asked me if I would mind if she called me Kaleb, and if I would call her Mrs. Roman. She asked me if I could cook. I told her I didn't know how, but that I would like to learn. Over the next two-and-a-half years she taught me how to cook. I would clean the house in the mornings and in the afternoons we would go walking in the park close to our house. On my day off I would visit Sam and play with little Anne. Life was good.

Then one day I went to see Sam at the store, and I found her talking to a boy I did not know. She told me his name was Paul and he had taken my job and was her new best freind and I was not to come around anymore. I said goodbye and left. On the way home, I started to cry. I felt broken hearted. When I got home, Mrs. Roman was sitting in the kitchen having some tea. She looked at me and saw I had been crying, and so she asked me what was troubling me. I told her that Sam had found a new boyfriend and that she had sent me away. She smiled at me and told me I would get over it. "You are a handsome young man, Kaleb," she said. "And you have the most striking blue eyes I have ever seen. The girls will be lining up to know you."

It made me feel a little better.

•—○○○—•

One day when Mrs. Roman was out, I desided to clean her room. I started with her closet. It was full of old, empty board boxes. I broke them down and carried them out to the trash then i found a cloth valise under some old cloths and looked in the valise. Inside it was full of bundles of money. I could not count too good, but I knew it was a lot of money, and so I put it back in the closet where I found it and thought no more about it.

One morning Mrs. Roman found me working in the kitchen and said her lawyer was coming for lunch and would I mind going to the market for something to serve him. I walked to a new market a few blocks in the other direction from the old one because I did not want to see Sam anymore. Then I picked out some German sausages and fresh vegetables and fruit, and then I stopped at the bakery for fresh buns and small cakes that I knew Mrs. Roman liked. When the lawyer came I showed him into the parlor and Mrs. Roman said I could serve lunch. I served lunch with a large pot of sweet tea. After lunch they spent the afternoon in the study. Late in the day they called me into the study and told me they had been making out Mrs. Roman's last will and testament and that they wanted me to witness the papers. I could not write, but I could sign my name. When I was finished, she told me I was mentioned in her will. I did not know what that meant, and so I thought no more about it until one morning three months later on returning from the market I saw a group of people standing outside our house. When I got close I saw a nurse at the front door, so I rushed up and pushed my way through into the house. A doctor inside the house asked me what I wanted. I told her I lived here and asked her what was going on. She told me Mrs. Roman had a heart attack and was very sick and that they were getting ready to go to the hospital next door. When they left with Mrs. Roman, I followed, but they stopped me and told me to come back after supper to see her. At home I tried to eat supper, but I could not, and so I walked through the house until it was time to go to the hospital to see Mrs. Roman. When I got there they told me she had died. I went home and cried my heart out. That's when I knew I really loved her as a mother.

Her lawyer came the next morning and told me he was sending Mrs. Roman back to England where she was born to rest in the family plot in London. He told me he had called the president of the hospital to a meeting in the afternoon and that I was to be there, too, so he could read Mrs. Roman's last will and testament. At one o'clock they came and I served them cakes and sweet tea in the parlor. After tea, the lawyer opened the will and told the president that they would receive the house and the property that it was on as well as a large some of money. As for me, I would receive the contents of the house. The lawyer for his long years of loyal service to her would receive all her remaining interests and properties around the world. He told me that I had thirty days to sell the contents, because after that time what was left in the loth house would belong to the hospital. When the lawyer left he told me he would be back in the morning to help me sell the contents.When I was alone, I went to Mrs. Roman's room and looked in the closet. The cloth valise was still there, so I took it out and put it on the bed and opened it. The money was still there,so I took the valise outside and found a good hiding place for it, and I spent the rest of the night crying for Mrs. Roman.

I went into her room and found a box on her dresser and opened it and found five rings with diamonds in them, so I put them in my pocket as a reminder of her.

The next morning the lawyer came to help me sell the contents. He had sent word to his rich friends that I was having a sale and a large group of them showed up and bought everything in the house except my personal belongings. When we counted the money from the sale he said we did very well and gave me 3,200 dollars. I asked him if I had to pay him for helping me and he laughed and said that Mrs. Roman had already payed him to help me. He left, and I packed my clothes in a small, cloth valise I had set aside and went and got the cloth valise I had hidden outside. With the two valises and 3,200 dollars in my pockets I was on my way to somewhere better, though to exactly where, I did not know.

Chapter 3

The Train

I WAS STANDING OUTSIDE MRS. ROMAN'S HOUSE NOT knowing which way to go when I heard a train whistle off to my left. I walked towards the sound and came to a train station and went in. I saw a man in a uniform and went up to him and asked him how I could get a ride on the train. He looked at me, then asked me where I was going. I did not know, so I told him south. He looked in the book he had and told me the next train south was going to St. Louis, and I needed a ticket. He pointed to a ticket booth. I went over to it and asked the man in the booth for a ticket to St. Louis. The man told me it would cost me ten dollars one way. I paid him and he gave me a ticket and said the train to St. Louis would be here soon and would come in on Platform Number One. I had a short wait, and so I went to a shop next to the station and bought two sandwiches and a bottle of milk, then sat on a bench to wait for the train.

The St. Louis train came in on time and let some passengers off, so I walked up to the man standing at the steps of the train and showed him my ticket. He looked at it, and then told me to get on and find a seat. When I came through the door, a black man in a white uniform looked at my ticket and told me for a dollar more I could have a padded seat in the front of the car and that I should sit facing the front of the train so I would not get sick like sailors did. I did not know what he meant, and so I found a seat facing front and sat down. He told me he was a porter and I could call him Rosco and that he would look after my bags. I told him I would look after them myself and thanked him for his kindness. He told me if I needed anything to call him. I was sitting there for only a few minutes when a young man in a suit came down the aisle and stopped at my seat and asked if he could sit with me. I looked at him and said "yes," and so he sat down and told me he was George Brown and held out his hand. I told him my name and shook his hand and we rode in silence for a while. Then George told me he had been in school in Chicago and was now a Geologist. I asked him what a Geologist was and so for the next two hours he told me about how to find gold and gem stones. This interested me and I kept asking him questions until he fell asleep. It was a pleasant two days to Springfield, Illinois where we had to change trains to St. Louis, which took another two days to get to.

When we arrived, George told me he had to wait for his ride out to the gold mine where he would be working. I walked over to the ticket window and asked the man where the next train south was going and when. He looked at his papers then said the next train south was to Tulsa,

Oklahoma with a stop in Springfield, Missouri and that it would be here in about two hours. George and I went for lunch, and then to a bookstore George had found, there he bought a book on gemology. We walked back to the station to wait. We sat on a bench and john showed me the book. It had pictures of gem stones and gold mines. When his ride came, he gave me the book and said it might come in handy someday. I thanked him and shook his hand and wished him well on his new job. Little did I know our paths would cross later in my life. I still had a wait for my train, and so I went out of the station and walked along the street. It was crowded with people and wagons going everywhere fast. I found a bench and sat down and watched the people go by and I thought to myself 'I could not live like this.'

About the time I thought my train would be coming, I walked back to the station to find my train indeed coming into the station. When the train stopped, passengers got off, and then I got on. I had to sit with two old miners all the way from St. Louis to Springfield. I listened to their stories of goldrushes and how they were going to find the motherload. I did not know what a motherload was, but I thought it must be something good by the way they talked about it.

They got off at Springfield. I slept most of the way to Tulsa, Oklahoma with my valise as a pillow. I was awakened by a porter. He was holding my valise. He told me a man had tried to steal it and that he had taken it from him and had thrown him off the moving train. I did not know how to thank him, so I took out a five-dollar bill and gave it to him and thanked him very much. His face lit up, and he said it was a pleasure. It had been eight days since I had left Chicago and I wondered to myself how big this country really was. At Tulsa a young woman got on and asked if I would mind if she sat with me. I looked at her and saw a beautiful face with wide green eyes and a gentle smile. I could not say no, and so I moved my valises and put them under my seat. She sat down and told me her name was Alice Devon. I told her mine and shook her hand. She told me she was going home to Dallas Texas because her parents had been killed in a buggy accident. For the next seven days we talked a lot. Each day the train would stop for water and wood and a lady would come on board with sandwiches and cold milk for sale. After three days, Alice told me that she had run out of money, so I bought extra sandwiches and milk for us and she thanked me. On the fifth day she told me that her father had sent her away to have a baby because she was only seventeen and not married. A tear came to her eyes when she told me her baby had died at birth. She also told me she did not know where the father was because he had worked for her father, and he had sent him away, too. We talked a lot about ranching and farming, and I told her about myself and said I did not know where I was going next. We had to change trains at McAlistre Oklahoma for Dallas Texas. The Dallas train was waiting for us to come in, and it was a rush from one train to the other. Once we we were seated on the Dallas train, it pulled out.

"I have no idea what I'll find when I get home," Alice said. " Would you like to come to my ranch for a while. In fact, you can stay as long as you want."

"I would like that very much, but I'm gonna have to leave when the time comes."

"That's all right with me, Kaleb. I just hope you're always honest."

We arrived in Dallas in the morning. Alice said she had not told anyone she was coming. I told her I would see if I could find a buggy to take us out to the ranch. I asked her to stay at the station with our bags until I came back. I went looking for a livery stable and found one two blocks from the train station and when in to talk to the man there. He asked me what I wanted so I told him I was looking for a buggy to rent for a week or more. He looked at me for a minute and then asked me where I was going with his buggy. I told him I wanted to take Miss Alice Devon out to her ranch. His face lit up. He told me he knew her father, and so I told him her mother and father were dead. His face went white and he sat down. Then he asked how they had died, and so I told him what Alice had told me. After a few minutes, he told me he had a buggy I could use but that it would cost me ten dollars for the week, and I would have to leave a deposit of fifty dollars that I would get back when I brought the buggy back. I paid him and said I would go and get Alice and be right back . When I got back to the station, Alice was standing where I left her with our bags. I told her I had found a buggy. We carried our bags over to the livery stable and went in. The livery man told Allice he had known her father and was sorry to hear he was dead. They talked while I put the bags in the buggy. When she was finished talking I helped her up onto the buggy seat and I said goodbye to the livery man and we were off. We stopped at a bakery that sold hot food and had our breakfast. Then I stopped at a mercantile store and bought a warm coat and a pair of boots and a strong duffle bag to put my valise full of money in. I asked Alice if she needed anything. She said "no" so she showed me the road to take to her ranch.

Chapter 4

The Ranch

WE ARRIVED AT THE RANCH IN THE AFTERNOON. I COULD
see that it was in bad shape with some fencing down and
the house in need of work. I stopped the buggy at the front
door of the house and Alice got down and went into the
house. Meanwhile, I drove the buggy to the barn and got
down and went inside. In the back I found an old Mexican
asleep in the hay. I kicked his boot and he jumped up with
a start. He looked at me and asked me what I wanted. I
asked him what he was doing.

"I work here on this ranch. I am called Poco. Who are you?
I told him my name then added: "And I've brought Alice
Devon home,"

His face lit up as he asked me where she was. I told him
she was in the house. He rushed passed me and out the door
to meet Alice coming from the house. He picked her up in
his arms. She kept saying his name over and over until he

put her down and held her at arms' length and laughing said, "You came home!"

Alice laughed back at him and said, "Yes, I have. Now, tell me what happened at the my ranch. "

Poco shook his head and told her that after her parents died, the ranch hands left, but he stayed to look after the place, hoping she would come home. He told us he had sold the cattle one at a time to keep the ranch going and that he sold the last steer a week ago. Alice said she was glad he had stayed and that she was not angry at him for selling the cattle. She hugged him again and told him she was glad to be home. She then told Poco about meeting me on the train, and how I had offered to help her and that I would be staying on the ranch for a while. Poco smiled at me. "I was here on the ranch long long before Miss Alice was born, and I watched her grow into a fine young lady."

At the end of the week, I told Alice I had to take the buggy back to Dallas and I asked her if would she like to come with me. She said she would stay at the ranch, and so I took the buggy back and asked the livery man if he knew where I could buy a wagon and a team of horses. He thought about it for a minute then said he did, but it would take a day to arrange. While I waited I went to the mercantile store and placed an order for the supplies I thought we would need and told the clerk I would be back the next day. I went back to the livery stable and the man said he had a good wagon and team of young horses for me, and they would be here in the morning. They would cost me two hundred dollars. I told him the price was all right and could he put me up for the night. He said I could sleep in the hay loft, and so I went for a walk around town and found a dining room in the hotel and had my supper. Then I went back to the livery stable and talked to the man for a while. Then I went to sleep in the hayloft.

The next morning the wagon and team of horses came to the livery. I looked them over and told the man they would do nicely and paid him and shook his hand. Then I drove over to the mercantile store to pick up my supplies. I helped the clerk load them on the wagon and paid him one hundred dollars. That afternoon I arrived back at the ranch and pulled the wagon up to the house and called Poco, who was staying close to Alice, to come help me unload the wagon. Alice came with him and she looked at the team of horses and the wagon load of supplies.

"Now whatever is going on. Where did all these supplies come from?"

I told her about Mrs. Roman and the money she had left me in her will. She smiled at me and said thank you. For the next six months Poco and I mended fences and made repairs to the barn and Alice cleaned and painted the inside of the house. Alice turned out to be a good cook and she would cook us a special Sunday supper. Poco and I liked her dinners a lot and we outdid each other with compliments on her cooking skills.

One day, when I was getting the wagon ready to go to Dallas for supplies, Poco said he had never been to Dallas, and so I asked Alice if she would like to go with us to Dallas. She said she would like that. So we went to Dallas and stayed in a hotel. Poco had a great time seeing things he had only dreamed about. Alice asked me if she could pick out some cloth to make curtains for the house, and so we went to the mercantile store. While she looked at the different patterns they had, I bought Poco new clothes and a new pair of boots. That night I treated them to a good supper and we found a theatre with actors putting on a show. Alice thought it was wonderful, but Poco looked at me and rolled his eyes. I smiled at him. From that day on, I had to take him with me when I went to Dallas or he would sulk around the ranch for days.

One day a rider came by to say hello. He told me he owned the ranch next to the Devon ranch. He told me his name was Sam Walsh and put out his hand. I told him my name and shook his hand. He then said he was a good friend to the Devons and was sorry to hear of their death. I asked him to stay for lunch and Sam and Alice talked about old times. After lunch Sam asked me to come and have a visit at his ranch. I told him I would and off he went. So one day, not long after Sam's, visit I rode over to his ranch. He smiled when he saw me and shook my hand. He then showed me around his ranch. I could see he was proud of it. We walked over to the corral and watched a cowboy working with a horse. When he saw us standing there he came over to us. Sam introduced him to me saying he was Jim Todd, his best hand. I told him my name and shook his hand. He asked me what ranch I had come from and I said the Devon Ranch. He asked me if I had bought the Devon Ranch. I laughed and said, "No, I only worked for the owner Alice Devon."

"You her husband?"

"No, sir."

"How long Miss Alice been home," Todd asked.

"About a year."

"You know what happened to her baby?"

"The baby died, right there at birth," I said.

A sadness came over his face, and then he told me he was the baby's father. We talked for a while. When I was ready to leave I asked him if he would like to come for lunch at our ranch on Sunday. He said he would be over at noon and waved good bye as I rode away. When I got back to our ranch, I found Alice in the kitchen making pies. She had flour on her face and was humming to herself. I told her we were going to have a guest for Sunday lunch. She looked at me, and so I told her it was someone I had met today. She said that would be all right. I asked her to sit down for a minute, that I had a ranch matter I wanted to talk to her about. She sat down and hugged herself and a sad look came over her face.

I said, "Don't look so sad, it's a good thing, I hope." She relaxed a little, and so I asked her what she thought about me buying into the ranch.

She laughed with relief. "As far as I'm concerned you already own half."

I told her, "No I do not." And asked her again what she thought would be a fair price. She said she did not know and would leave that up to me to come up with a fair price. The next day I rode over to a ranch that had some young steers for sale and told the rancher I was Kaleb Jakobs from the Devon Ranch and that I was looking for some start-up stock. He told me he was Fred Johnson and that I had come to the right place and shook my hand. He showed me what he had for sale. I picked out forty cows and a young bull and four riding ponies and two big wagon horses. After a short time of haggling we came to a price of one thousand dollars cash. I counted out his money and realized I only had about three hundred dollars left of the money from Mrs. Roman's contents sale. I told Fred I would pick up the stock in a weeks time. At supper that night I told Alice about the stock I had bought for the ranch. She smiled at me and said that with all the money I had spent on the ranch and the new stock it was a fair price, and the next time we went to Dallas she would have me sign the papers for half the ranch. Then she looked at Poco. He was beside himself with excitement that we had a working ranch again.

That Sunday was a warm and clear day. My guest arrived at noon. I met him at the corral and shook his hand. He was all shined up with a big smile on his face. I walked with him to the house and we went in through the kitchen door. I said hello and it startled Alice, who was putting the finishing touches to lunch. She looked up and smiled at me, then stopped. Her face went white. She hugged herself and stared at the man standing beside me.

Jim said, "Hello, Alice, long time no see."

Alice started to cry, and so Jim walked over to her and wrapped his arms around her and started to cry, too. I nodded to Poco, who was sitting at the table and we went outside to wait and see what would happen next. A short time later they came out and looked out over the ranch and finally told us lunch was ready. As we walked through the door, Alice whispered to me "thank you."

At lunch Alice and Jim talked about what had happened to them after her father had sent them away. It was a long lunch. Poco and I sat and listened to their stories and enjoyed them. When Jim was ready to leave they promised each other to get together again real soon.

I walked Jim to the corral to get his horse and asked him if he could help me drive my new stock from Mr. Johnson's ranch. He said he would help and if Alice made some pies he would bring extra help.

The next Saturday morning Jim showed up with four men, so we went over to Fred Johnson's ranch and drove my new stock back to our ranch. The four men made quick work of a pie each. Poco was so happy to have cattle on the ranch again. After lunch Jim asked Alice and me if he could come and work on our ranch and Alice said yes.

The next day Jim showed up with his gear and Alice showed him a room next to mine. A month later we hired a cowboy who had worked with Jim to help with the stock so Jim could spend more time breaking in the riding ponies. Alice and Jim got real close and at a Sunday dinner later that month Jim asked Alice to marry him, period.

She looked at him. "It took you long enough. And, yes. I will marry you."

Alice asked me to take her to Dallas so she could buy material to make a wedding dress, and so Jim said he would stay on the ranch while we went to town; he did not want Poco to sulk around the ranch for weeks and laughed. So Alice, Poco and I went to town, and I bought her a very nice wedding dress and a suit for Poco and myself. Then we went to the mercantile store for a wagon full of supplies and at Christmas Alice and Jim got married. A minister came and stayed over Christmas with us and some of Jim's friends came and Poco gave the bride away and a long-time friend of Jim's stood up with him. We all had a good time and I paid for them to have a week-long honeymoon in Dallas.

That winter we sold some of our mature cattle and bought more young stock and we had to hire a man to help put up more fencing. I could see the ranch was going to make it just fine. The winter turned into spring. One day I found Alice in the kitchen making pies and asked her if I could talk to her. She looked at me and started to cry. I told her now that she was married to Jim and the ranch was doing just fine it was time for me to move on. She cried harder, and so I got up and went to her and hugged her until she stopped crying. I asked her to remember what she had said back on the train on our way to Dallas.

"You told me that I could stay as long as I wanted, Alice. Well the time has come for me to move on."

She looked so sad, and so I said I would stay for a month. For the next month Alice would cry every time she looked at me; it was all Jim could do to comfort her. The day before I left, I told Jim and Alice that any profit that was coming to me was to be put back into the ranch. That night I put a thousand dollars in an envelope and in the morning at our last breakfast together I gave the envelope to Alice. She opened the envelope and started to cry. Jim took it from her and looked inside, and then looked at me with a question on his face. I told him the ranch was my home and the money had been given to me by Mrs. Roman, and I knew they would put it to good use. Jim thanked me and said I would always have a home here and shook my hand

and gave me a big hug and I told him to look after Alice and the ranch. Then I gave Alice a big hug and kissed her and said I would always love her. Then I kissed her again and went out to get my horse. Poco was holding my horse. I gave him a big hug, then shook his hand and told him to look after Alice and Jim, and that I would miss him a lot. Then I got on my horse and said goodbye again and rode down the trail west. After a few minutes I looked back to see the three of them standing on the porch watching me go. Tears came to my eyes and a pain stabbed through my heart. The ranch had been a real home to me, and they had been a real family to me, and I would miss them all for the rest of my life.

Chapter 5

Wagon Trains

I RODE WEST FOR THREE DAYS, SLEEPING UNDER THE STARS and thinking about what I had left behind and about what I would find in the future. I was nineteen years old and did not know where I was going and it felt good. On the fourth day I came to a town called Fort Worth Texas . The first thing I did was head to the livery stable and have the man there give my horse a good rub down and pail of oats. While my horse was being looked after I went looking for a bath house for a bath and a shave. Feeling much better, I looked for a place to get a hot meal and found a small saloon that sold hot food. While I was eating I overheard two men talking about a supply train getting ready to leave town going west, and so I went looking for the wagon master to see if I could get a ride with them and found the wagon master talking to a group of men. When he was finished I walked up to him and asked if I could get a ride west. He looked at me and said he did not take any passengers, but

I could work my way west. He told me he was looking for a cook's helper. It paid dollar a week and all I could eat. I said I would take the job and so he told me to be ready to leave in the morning to take supplies to Abelene, Texas. That night I stayed at the hotel and in the morning I went to the wagon train and the wagon master introduced me to a miserable old Mexican cook who only grunted at me, and so I cut wood and washed pots and dishes and worked hard and the cook took a liking to me and started to show me how to cook for a big gang of hard-nosed teamsters, and how to bake bread in a thing he called a Dutch oven, a square metal box you put on the side of the fire until it gets quite hot. Soon we were getting along just fine. Seven days out of Fort Worth our horses pulling the chuck wagon were spooked by a rattle snake and took off running. The chuck wagon flipped over, throwing me off and I landed on the ground with a lot of pain in my arm and the side of my face. The cook hung onto the wagon and broke his back and died that afternoon. Two drivers dug his grave, and the wagon master said some words over him, and they filled in the grave, and then a driver made a marker and hammered it into the ground to mark the grave.

•————○○○————•

After this was done, the wagon master took me aside and said I was now the cook and I was not to poison any of his men and walked away laughing. We spent the rest of the day fixing the chuck wagon and repacking it, making it ready for the trail. The cook had made a stew so I fed it to the men with fresh bread and things were okay. The next morning they sent me a young man to be my helper. The first meals were not so good, and the wagon master came by and told me to put more salt in the food to make it fit to eat. I never got good at it, and I never made friends with any of the teamsters.

One day I made biscuits, and they turned out badly. One of the men threw his biscuit at me. I ducked and it hit my helper in the eye and that eye was black for two weeks. So, for the rest of the trip so I kept a strong stick in the wagon. I only had to show it once and the man backed off, and I had no more trouble from them. For the next three weeks I kept the food simple and hot.

We arrived in Abelene, Texas in the evening tired and dirty, and I told the wagon master that I was leaving. He shook my hand and said I had done a good job and that made me feel better. I went into town and found a hotel room and had a much needed bath and haircut. Abelene was a fair-sized town with wagon trains coming and going every week. After a fine steak and biscuits and gravy, I went back to the hotel and fell asleep in a real bed.

In the morning I opened the valise to make sure the money was still there. That's when I found a letter I had not seen before. I opened it and saw my name on it. I could not read, but I saw Mrs. Roman's name at the bottom, and I knew it was for me. Right then, I promised myself I would learn to read and write, and then I put the letter back into the valise.

I had used up all the money from the sale at Mrs. Roman's house and so I took out a small amount of money and closed the valise and put it back in my duffel bag. I could not believe I had carried it halfway across the country and no one knew about it. After breakfast, I went looking for a mercantile store and bought some new clothes and a new hat and carried them back to my hotel room and put them on. I walked the streets of Abelene for a while and got hungry, so I looked for a place to eat and found a café and went in for lunch. While I was eating, I wondered what I was going to do next and where I would go. I overheard two men at the next table talking about a wagon train that had just come to town. One of them said the wagon train had been attacked by Mexican bandits and some of the wagons had been burnt and two men had been killed and they were looking for two men to drive the dead men's wagon, or they would have to stay behind. I thought I might get a job driving one of the wagons, and so I finished my lunch and went looking for the wagon train and found the wagon master and told him I had just come off a supply train as a cook and was looking for a ride west. He told me he had two wagons that needed drivers and if I wanted he would take me to see them. I told him I would like that, so he took me to see the first wagon. I found it in bad shape and the horses old and tired. Not only that, the lady had two daughters that looked like trouble, so I told him I would pass on this one. Then he took me over to the second wagon. At first I thought I was looking at a young boy, but after talking to her for a few minutes I could see she was a good-looking girl who talked and acted tough but had the manners of a lady. The wagon master told her I had come to talk to her about driving her wagon, and she told me if she could not get a driver to help her she would have to stay behind and she had come too far to stop now, and I saw a tear in her eye. She told me her name was Jane, and what did they call me when it was raining. I laughed and told her my name. She asked me what I wanted for driving her wagon, and so I told her a good meal and a dry place to sleep. While she talked to the wagon master, I took a look at her wagon and team of horses and found them sound, and so I went back to them and she said a good meal and a bed under her wagon. I smiled at her and said it was a fair deal, and so that night she cooked a good stew and biscuits and hot coffee and we talked about the road ahead until the fire burned out. Then I made my bed under the wagon and went to sleep.

The next morning while we were eating our breakfast, Jane told me how her father had been killed by the bandits and her wagon had been robbed and how they had taken most of her money. We were drinking the last of the pot of coffee when the wagon master came by to tell us we would be leaving in two days and to put on extra water because the trail over to our next stop, Loraine Texas, would be long and dry with rough spots and a small mountain range to cross and the pass riddled with bandits, who often attacked the wagon trains.

"You got any guns?" he asked.

"No, not a one," I said.

"Well, you best get some in town."

I admitted then that I'd never fired a gun in my life.

"Guess it's time you learned. I'll show ya," he said.

That night I asked Jane if she could read and write. She smiled at me and said she could. I told her I had not gone to school and could not read or write and could she teach me. She said she would try. The next morning I woke to the smell of food cooking. At breakfast I asked Jane if she were going to town for supplies. She said 'no,' that she did not have any money and that we have to do with what she had. I asked her to make out a list of the supplies we would need. She gave me her list. I noted that it was small. I knew we needed a lot more supplies. In town I went to the mercantile store and asked the clerk to double everything on the list and anything he thought we would need and to put in two large coils of strong rope. The clerk looked at my order and told me it was a large order and that he would need help. Off he went. In a short time he came back with an older man who told me he was Hiram Jakobs and he was the owner. I told him I was Kaleb Jakobs and shook his hand. He looked at me, and then asked me where I was from, and so I told him, "Chicago Illinois,"

He laughed. "That is a fair coincidence. I hail from Chicago, too."

I told him my father was Farley Jakobs from Hebron Illinois and he laughed harder and told me he was Farley's cousin and that made me his cousin, too. He shook my hand and said, "Welcome to Loraine Texas." He looked at my order and said it was a large order and would cost a lot of money.

"How much," I asked.

He counted everything up and said about two hundred dollars. I told him that was all right and took out my money and paid him. He told the clerk to fill my order and asked me to follow him into his office for coffee. We talked for a long time about our families.

"I allow I never liked your father much," he said.

"I didn't like my father at all," I replied.

He said he had left home when he was young because Farley had gotten him into some trouble, and so he came south to find a life for himself and landed here in Loraine Texas and stayed.

When my order was ready, I asked the clerk if he could find a wagon to take my order out to the wagon camp. He said he could, and it would cost me five dollars. I told him that was all right and could he hold the wagon until I got back because I had more to put with my order. At that I went looking for a gun shop and found one next to the livery stable. And so I took my horse in for a good rub-down and a pail of oats. Then I went into the gun shop and found the clerk behind his counter reading a newspaper. He looked up when I entered and asked me if he could help me. I told him I was looking for some guns. He laughed and said I had come to the right place. "What kind of guns did you have in mind," he asked.

I told him I did not know anything about guns and maybe he could help me. He smiled at me and asked me what I was going to shoot with the guns.

"Looks like Mexican bandit," I said.

He nodded his head and showed me some hand guns in a glass case. I looked at them and told him I had never held a gun before, and so he took one out of the case and handed it to me. It felt good—heavy and sleek. I asked him how to use it. He said it was a Colt .45 and he showed me how to load it and how to clean it. "Be careful, now. Don't shoot your foot off."

I asked him how much he wanted for it. He thought for a minute then said forty dollars and for five dollars more he would throw in a holster and a box of shells. I spotted a smaller hand gun in the glass case and asked him about it. He told me it was made for a woman and I could have it for thirty dollars.

Then he showed me a Winchester repeating rifle. I liked the feel of it, so I bought two of them. Now I had two hand guns and two rifles. He then gave me a nice hunting knife and extra boxes of ammunition. I asked him if he would mind taking them over to the mercantile store for the Kaleb Jakobs' order. He looked at me, and I told him I was Hiram Jakob's cousin. He smiled at me and said he was Hiram's best friend in town and that he'd be pleased to take the guns over to the mercantile store. I thanked him and went to get a bath and a shave, and then some lunch. When I came out of the café I spotted a school house at the end of the street and headed that way. As I went along I came to a shop that sold dress making materials, and so I went in and found a roll of gingham cloth and some coloured ribbons for Jane's hair. I carried my packages back to the mercantile store and told the clerk to send my order out to the wagon park to Jane's wagon. I went to say goodbye to cousin Hiram and told him I would look him up the next time I was in town.

He shook my hand and said it was grand meeting me. Then I went and got my horse at the livery stable and rode over to the school and knocked at the back door. A middle-aged woman opened the door and asked me what I wanted. I told her my name and asked her if I could talk to her for a minute.

"School is out for the day. But you're welcome to come in,"

When we were sitting at a table I told her I had not gone to school and did not know how to read or write and a woman on our wagon train was going to teach me. "What I'm asking, I guess, is if you have some old school books I might purchase."

She got up and went to a cupboard and came back with a crate full of books and writing materials. I asked her how much she wanted for them. She said they were old and I could have them for free, but if I wanted I could make a donation to the school fund. And so I took out a twenty-dollar gold piece and pressed it into her hand. She smiled at me and thanked me.

Chapter Six

Learning to Read

I ARRIVED BACK AT CAMP TO FIND THE WAGON FROM TOWN unloading our supplies, so I helped the man finish the job and gave him five dollars for his wagon and a dollar for him and then I thanked him. He left. After the wagon was out-of-sight, Jane stood there looking a little angry. I asked her what was bothering her. She said it cost a lot of money for the supplies and what was I expecting from her for them. I smiled at her and said she had promised to teach me how to read and write and that was all, and I got the crate of books and showed her. I did not think she believed me, so I said I could take them back. She laughed and said it was all right. I told her my cousin Hiram owned the mercantile in town and I think she felt better. After supper, I looked after the horses and Jane got out a first grade book and showed me how to recognize the alphabet. She asked me if I would mind if some of the people on the wagon train learned along with me. I said it would be all right, and so the next evening three young adults came over and we worked together and it made learning a fun game. Every spare minute we would get together. I think Jane liked the group because each week we were getting better and we all felt good about it. The next morning, I hooked the horses to our wagon and started out.

After three days on the trail, the wagon master took Jane and I and anyone who did not know how to shoot a gun out into the desert and showed us how to handle our guns. Jane would laugh when she hit the target and I missed, but it did not take long for me to get good at it. It took us three weeks of rough going to get to the mountain pass, and then we started a slow climb up to the pass. Halfway up it started to rain. It rained for the four days it took us to get to the top. At one point we had to hook up extra teams of horses to pull the wagon through the mud. By the time we got to the top we all were played out and wet to our skin. We found a flat area and made camp and, then the rain stopped. We stayed there for two days to dry out our gear and to give the horses a well-deserved rest, and we had our first hot meal in four days. It tasted better than anything. Some of the wagons had to be repaired, and so all the men got together and made the work go faster with lots of laughter. We had to unload our wagon to replace some floor boards that had broken on the way up the pass, and then we repacked it so Jane could have a little more sleeping room. It was a two-week run down to Big Spring Texas. When we got there the wagon master told us it was a long dry run to our next stop, Andrews Texas, and so we added extra water barrels to our wagons.

We stayed in Big Spring for three days. There our little reading group practiced and Jane started to teach us how to write. In a very short time we started to get good at it. Jane would have us copy a book, and then have us read it to her and she would laugh and clap her hands when we got it right. We left Big Spring on a Monday morning and it was clear and warm, so Jane got out a book and started to read it to me. I liked it, and so when it was her turn to drive I would read to her. She would laugh each time I made a mistake, and all that reading made the days go by faster.

Thirty miles from Lenora Texas we came to a river we had to cross. It was not very wide but deep in places, and so we cut down some large trees we found along the river bank and, as each wagon came up to cross, we would tie a tree log to each side of the wagon to help it float. And then we tied a rope to the front of the wagon and several men went across with their horses and the rope to help pull the wagon across. We tied a rope to the back of the wagon and two men on horseback held the rope to keep the wagon from drifting down the river. We piled the food on top of our gear in the wagons to keep it dry. It was very hard work, and it took us two days to get all the wagons across. We only lost one wagon. The horses hooked to that wagon got spooked and started to thrash about in the water and the wagon flipped over. The men holding the ropes could not save it, but the horses broke free from the wagon tree and were saved. We found space on the wagons for the family, and we stayed there for a day to rest and dry out any gear that got wet.

That evening while we were eating our supper, two men got into a fight about how one of them was treating his family. They shot and killed each other. We buried them by the side of the trail, and then I drove one of the dead men's wagons on into Andrews Texas.

We stayed there for two days while the wagon master found two men to drive the driverless wagons to our next stop, Carlsbad New Mexico. We needed supplies, and so I took Jane into andrews . The first stop was the bath house. It was the first hot water we had in months and it felt good. Then I got my hair cut and a shave. Jane came out of the bath house with her hair hanging down. It looked so nice that way. I then took her to the hotel for lunch. We had a big steak each with fresh biscuits and gravy and lots of hot coffee. After lunch we went over to the mercantile store for supplies. At the door Jane stopped me and said I had paid for all the supplies from the time I had offered to drive her wagon. "Where did all that money come from," she asked all solemn.

so I told her about the money I had gotten from the sale of Mrs. Roman's house, and how I would be ever-grateful to her for teaching me how to read and write. "It makes me feel good to help," I added.

She said no more and went into the store and ordered the supplies we would need. Later that day Jane asked me to read a new book to her that she had found in town. When I was finished reading it to her, she smiled at me and kissed me. I kissed her back. It made me feel real good, and so I climbed into the wagon and found the package I had been keeping from her and gave it to her. It was wrapped in oilcloth and tied with a string. She looked at the package and then at me. "Go on, open it," I said.

She untied the string and a hair ribbon fell out. She looked then at the roll of gingham cloth and started to cry. She touched the cloth with trembling fingers and, between sobs, said it was beautiful. Then she kissed me again, and so I took her in my arms and kissed her back. I was pleased the gift made her feel happy, and I thought she must feel the same way I did when Mr. Ned gave me the knife for my birthday. That night it got very cold and Jane said in a quiet voice that I could sleep in the wagon if I wanted. I smiled at her and said that would be nice. The next morning we smiled at each other as we packed up our campsite. We got ready to get on the trail, and travelled west from Andrews for about ten days and came to a town called Eunice, New Mexico.

We saw smoke long before we got there and some of us who had riding horses rode over to town to see what was going on. When we rode into town someone took a shot at us, and so we put up our hand to show we were friendly. Just then, a man with a gun stepped out from an alley and asked us who we were. One of our group told him we were from a wagon train and that we'd seen the smoke and that we came to see what was going on. He told us the town had been raided by a gang of Mexican bandits and that they had killed the sheriff and the bank manager and four town's people while robbing the bank and the mercantile store. The men in town had cornered some of the bandits and had killed three of them and wounded two more. The rest of the bandits were spread out around town and had set fire to some of the buildings to cover their escape. We helped them put out the fires and bury the dead, then we went back to our wagons and pulled them into a circle, and the wagon master called a meeting with all the people to tell us to be very careful and keep our guns ready, and We would take turns standing guard at night. We stayed in Eunice for a week to help the town recover from the attack, but we did not see any more bandits.

When we were ready to leave, the whole town came out to see us off. It was quite a show and it made my heart beat a little faster to see the children from town running alongside our wagons shouting goodbye. From that point on we were on extra guard: men with rifles at the ready and women with handguns and shotguns. The wagon master had told us our next stop would be Carlsbad New Mexico, and that it would be the hardest part of the whole trip west given the many places for bandits to hide and ambush us. A week out of Eunice we were attacked by a large group of Mexican bandits who shot up our wagon train and wounded several people and killed a few horses, but our firepower surprised them and, after a short battle, they rode away carrying their wounded. We saw them several times after that, but they did not come close.. The trail to Carlsbad was mountainous and very rough, and we had to stop many times to repair broken wheels and once to dig a grave for a lady who fell out of her wagon and broke her neck. It was a sad time, and everyone came to say goodbye to her as we buried her in the rocky ground.

It took us three more weeks to get to Carlsbad. We were tired and dirty, and so after we made our camp, Jane and I went looking for a bathhouse. I got a hair cut and a shave, and then we went to the hotel for a good supper. The next morning, the wagon master called a meeting. He told us he thought it would be a good idea if we wintered the next two months in Carlsbad. Everyone agreed, and so we made a circle with our wagons and put up a rope corral for the horses. Four days later we held a dance. I danced most of the dances with Jane and drank lots of punch. We all had a good time. In the morning I woke up with a bad headache, Jane laughed at me and said I had a hangover and lots of strong coffee would help. After two cups of strong coffee I did feel better.

"What you going to do for these two months," I asked Jane

"The wagon master's asked me to run a school for the children, and I've said yes."

"I'm glad for you. I've never met a finer teacher," I told her, and then I hugged and kissed her. That night after Jane went to sleep, I lay awake thinking what it would be like spending the next two months in a wagon. I did not like what I saw. I knew I had to move on, and so I got up and wrote a letter to Jane, telling her how much I would miss her and thanking her for all the kindness she had showed me. Then I put two hundred dollars in the envelope with the letter and put it on my pillow and went and saddled my horse and rode to town. I was only there for a few minutes when I started to feel bad about what I had done, so I rode back to the camp and found Jane standing by the fire with my letter in her hand. I could see that she had been crying, so I got off my horse and walked over to her and hugged her for a long time. Then I let her go and she stepped back and smiled at me and told me she understood and would miss me a lot, and so I kissed her. Then I got on my horse and rode back into Carlsbad.

Chapter Seven

Hope

IN TOWN I BOUGHT SOME SUPPLIES AND RODE WEST. THE
trail turned north, and so I followed it After ten days on
the trail with a stop in a small place called Lakewood to
have a horseshoe replaced, I came to a town called Artesia,
which I later found out was the county seat. I was tired
and smelled worse than my horse, so I stopped at the only
hotel in town, which was no more than a big barn with
rooms and went in and asked the clerk for a room. He told
me I could have the best room in the place for two dollars
a night, and so I asked to see the best room he had and he
showed it to me. I looked at the room. "This here ain't a
room. It's a tent with a window."

"Fine. I'll take a dollar and a half"

"A dollar."

"Why not," he said and shrugged and gave me the key
to the room and left.

I locked the door, and thought that he got what he wanted in the first place. I put my gear away and went out to take my horse to the livery stable. I asked the man there to give my horse a good rub down and a pail of oats, and could he tell me if they had a bath house in town. He told me it was behind the hotel, so I walked back to the hotel and went around the back to find an old Chinese lady washing cloths. I asked her about a bath and a haircut. She pointed to a tent and bowed to me, and so I went in to find a big wooden tub half-full of almost-clean hot water. She told me twenty five cents for a bath and twenty five cents for a haircut. I waited for her to leave the tent, but she just stood there waiting for my cloths, so I took them off and handed them to her. She put her hand over her mouth and giggled to herself and left the tent. I got in the tub. The hot water felt so good. I was in the tub for about fifteen minutes when the old lady came in with a pair of scissors and a comb to cut my hair. When she was finished, she handed me a large towel. I knew my bath was over, and so I got out of the tub and wrapped the towel around myself. Then I asked her if she knew where I could get something to eat. She smiled at me and left the tent and was back in a few minutes with a tray full of small dishes of food, the like of which I had never seen before. I was so hungry I tried the food and found it tasted very good, and I finished all the food on the tray to the general merriment of the old lady. She took the food tray out and came back with my clothes all cleaned and pressed dry. I knew she was not going to leave, and so I dropped the towel and put my clothes on and asked her how much I owed her. She told me one dollar so I gave her two dollars and thanked her and told her I would be back for more of her cooking. She laughed and bowed to me and I left the tent. Later I found out the people in town called her Mama Son or China Lady. After my bath I went back to the livery stable to check on my horse. The man told me they had found gold in a place west of here called Almagordo and a group of prospectors were leaving town to go there. That evening I met a man who said he was going with them. I asked him if I could tag along. He told me to be ready when they left town in the morning, then we talked for hours. I liked his stories about finding gold, and I could have listened to him for hours more, but I had to get some sleep, and so I said my good night and went to my room.

When the group of prospectors left town I was with them. Everyone was talking about finding gold, and what they would do with the money they got for it, and everyone was in a good mood. A day west we came to a small town called Hope. The prospectors only stayed for two hours and left, but the man I was with had to have a horses-shoe replaced, and so I stayed with him.

I went for a walk around town and liked what I saw. That night the prospector and I got rooms in the hotel. After supper he told me how to pan for gold and what to look for, and said it was hard work and I might not find any, but if I did, it would be well worth the hard work. We talked well into the night. Finally I got tired and told him I was going to my room for some needed sleep. In the morning it was quite cold, and so I told the prospector I was going to stay in Hope for a while so he left to catch up with his friends. I could feel winter coming, so I walked over to the livery stable and asked the man there if he knew where I could get a room for the winter, and he said he did. I told him my name and. He said he was George Scott and shook my hand. He told me to go to the white house at the end of Main Street and tell the lady that George sent me.

I went and knocked at her door and a nice lady opened it and asked if she could help me. So I told her George at the livery stable said I might find a room for the winter. She asked me to come in and showed me to the kitchen and asked me to sit down. She asked me where I was from. I told her i was from Chicago but had lived for the last two years on a ranch in Dallas Texas.

She smiled at me. "My late husband's from Chicago. What was your name?" I told her, and she said I could call her Polly, because everyone in town did. She asked me if I would like some coffee and I said, "Yes, please, ma'am."

While we sipped our hot coffee she asked me how long I needed a room. I told her for two months or more. She told me a room in her house was three dollars a week with meals and asked me if I would like to see the room. I told her I surely would, and so she showed me a nice room on the second floor with a view up Main Street. I liked the room, and I told her I would take it and gave her ten dollars on account. Then I said I would go to the livery stable and get my gear and be right back in time for supper.

After supper I went to my room and locked the door and opened my duffle bag and took out the valise and counted the money and it came to 107,000 dollars and I could not believe I had carried that much money all the way from Chicago and no one even suspected. The next morning I took a good walk around town. It was small but growing, and I liked it because it gave me a warm feeling of being at home. They had two buildings half finished and they already had a hotel, a mercantile store, a livery stable, a bank, and a town hall with a sheriff's office and a jail beside it, and a row of nice houses on a side street, and Polly's boarding house at the end of Main Street. I walked over to the livery stable to see my horse and to talk to George. I told him I had come west to look for gold. He said the town was growing because they had found gold in the mountains in a place called Almagordo. I told him I was going with a gang of prospectors to Almagordo, but thought I would stay in Hope for the winter. He asked me if I had looked for gold before. I told him 'no.' He shook his head and laughed and told me he had come west looking for gold and in five years had found only enough gold to start his livery stable, and that this was where he was staying.

"How is it one goes about finding gold," I asked.

"You'll need a grubstake, first thing."

"What's a grubstake?"

He laughed. "Why, Kaleb, that's when someone puts up the money for the equipment you're gonna need to find all the gold."

I asked him what kind of equipment that would be.

He said I would need a good packhorse to carry the gear I would need, and a good tent to live in, and pots and pans, and a good shovel, and lots of food. I asked him what all this would cost. He said about two hundred dollars and he was willing to grubstake me for ten percent of what I found. I told him I would think about it and that I'd let him know later. I then went back to my boarding house and took out five thousand dollars and walked over to the bank and went in and asked a clerk if I could see the person in charge. The clerk walked into a back office and came out with a man in a grey suit and asked if he could help me. I told him my name and he said he was Bob Nelson and that this was his bank, and then he shook my hand. I told him I had just arrived in town and was staying at Polly's boarding house and that I had never been in a bank before and that I did not know how they worked. He smiled and asked me to follow him into his office. He asked me to sit down. "People put their money in my bank and I pay them a small interest and the more you put in the more interest you get paid."

"I like that. How would I go about putting money in your bank."

He told me once I had set up an account with his bank, I could give money to one of his clerks and they would write it in their book under my name.

I took out the five thousand dollars and put it on his desk. He looked at the money, then looked at me and asked me where I got the money from. I told him it was part of an inheritance I had received from Mrs. Roman back in Chicago. He picked up the money and counted it and said, "Five thousand dollars," and got out a book and wrote my name at the top of the page and wrote the amount on the first line. Then he picked a small book and said it was a cheque book and showed me how to use it. He said by using cheques I did not have to carry large amounts of money on me. I thanked him for his help and shook his hand, and he said if I needed any help to come and see him. On my way to the livery stable I touched my cheque book in my pocket and smiled to myself. I felt good, because at the age of nineteen I had a bank account. At the livery stable, I thanked George for his offer for a grubstake, but I had some money in the bank and could pay for my own grubstake and would he help me put one together. He said he would be pleased to and would keep an eye out for a good packhorse. Two weeks later, George told me he had found a strong pack horse, but that it would need some training, and I could have it for thirty dollars and ten dollars to train it. I took out my cheque book and wrote him a cheque for forty dollars. He laughed and said he had a cheque book, too. So, for the next two months, we talked about panning for gold and places to look for it. The weather got warm, and so I told George it was time for me to go prospecting and would he help me put together the gear I would need and show me how to use it, and he did and it was a fun time. When every thing was packed and ready to go I paid Polly three months' rent and asked her if she knew a safe place to put my valise because my valued possessions were in it. She thought for a minute, and then suggested I take it to the bank. I thought it a great idea, and so I took it over to the bank and asked Bob if I could put my valise in his safe while I was away prospecting. He said I could and wished me good luck. I walked back to Polly's and said goodbye. She smiled at me and said my room would be waiting for me when I came back. Then I walked over to the livery stable to pick up my gear. George had my pack horse ready, and so I shook his hand and he wished me well and told me to go west, because no one had found gold that way and he knew it was there.

Chapter 8

The Valley

I RODE WEST FOR THE BETTER PART OF A DAY WHEN I SAW some low mountains to the south and went to have a look and found a valley with mountains on three sides and a good stream running down the middle. One side of the valley was covered with large trees, and where the stream flowed out of the mountains it was rocky and covered with more trees. I rode up the valley and found a flat area among the trees with a grassy area by the stream for my horses. I set up my tent and made a rope corral to keep my horses from wandering away. Then I picked some small rocks out of the stream to make a fire pit. I built a fire and made some beans and pan biscuits and a pot of coffee. After supper I tended to my horses, then I sat by the fire until it burned out and then I looked out over the valley and liked what I saw. When it got dark I made my bed in the tent and went to sleep with my rifle by the bed.

In the morning the horses woke me with loud calls and stamping of their feet. I got up to see a large mountain cat in the rope corral about to attack my pack horses. I reached into the tent and got my rifle, and then took aim as the cat made a move towards my horse. I shot it in the hind end. The cat turned and looked at me, and then I shot it in the chest. It made a loud cry and fell over dead. The cat was the first thing I had ever shot, and I was shaking all over, and so I went to calm my horses, and then I dragged the heavy cat out of the coral. I went and started a fire and put on a pot of coffee and after a plate of cold beans and leftover biscuits I decided to skin the cat. I made a very bad job of it. I cut up some of the meat to eat and found it was not too bad, and so I cut some of the meat into strips and dried it over the fire to eat later. I hung the skin in a nearby tree, and then spent the rest of the day making my campsite liveable and then cooked the rest of the cat meat for later. The next morning the cat skin smelled so bad I had to dig a hole and bury it. I cut off the tail. It was a small tuff of fur that did not smell too bad. I spent the morning looking at the place the water came out of the mountain to form the stream and wondered where it came from. It was cold and clear and flowed down the valley to form a wide pond with lots of green grass around it. I went out each day for a week exploring the valley and did not see all of it. I thought it was the most beautiful place in the world, and I told myself I would like to own it all. The second week I started to look for gold and started to pan about half way up the stream and found no gold, and so I moved up the stream a little ways and tried again. This time I found a small trace of gold in the pan, and so I moved again and when the pan came out of the water I spied a small nugget sitting on a bed of fine gold. By the end of the afternoon I had a coffee cup full of gold. I could not believe my luck. I panned for gold for the rest of the week and ended up with a cloth coffee bag almost full of gold, and so I packed up my gear and rode back to town.

At my boarding house Polly told me she was glad to see me and said she had a spare room I could put my gear in and helped me put it away. About that time George showed up and said he had seen me come into town and he had come to see how I had made out. It was close to supper time, so Polly asked George to stay for supper, and he did. At supper I told them about the valley and the mountain cat I had killed and how much it stank. They laughed and George slapped me on my back, and so I took out the cat's tail and put it on the table. George picked it up and looked at it and then told us it was the closest he had ever come to a mountain cat, so I told him he could keep it. He showed it to Polly, and then put it in his pocket and smiled at me. After supper. I walked with George and my horses over to his livery. On the way, I showed him a large gold nugget I had found. He looked at it for a long time, and then told me it was a good one and the largest he had ever seen. so I told him he could keep it for helping me. He asked me if I had found the gold in the valley, and I told him I did. He smiled at me and said it was between us and no one else.

When we got to his livery I asked him what a person had to do to buy a place like the valley. He thought about it for a minute, and then said I would have to go over to the county seat in Artesia and have the land registered. So, the next morning after breakfast I walked over to the bank. This time when I walked in, Bob came out of his office and called me kaleb and shook my hand in front of his customers and invited me into his office and asked one of his clerks to bring us coffee. I sat down and and asked him for my valise and he got it out of his safe and handed to me then went out to talk to his clerk for a minute.when he came back i handed him five thousand dollars to put in my account.. When the coffee arrived, he came around his desk and sat in a chair beside me and asked me what my plans were, and so I told him about the valley I had found, and then I said I would like to buy it.

Bob told me I would have to go to Artesia and register the land. I said that George had told me the same thing and he laughed. He told me I would have to take a survey map of the land I wanted to buy with me when I registered the land. I asked him if he knew how to do a survey map. He said, 'no,' but he knew a surveyor that would do one for me.

That afternoon while I was taking a nap, a man came to the boarding house looking for me. Polly showed him into the parlor and came to my room and woke me up, saying I had a visitor in the parlour. When I entered the room he got up and told me he was John Brower and that Bob at the bank had told him I was looking for a surveyor. I told him my name and we shook hands, and then I asked him to sit down and asked Polly if she would mind bringing in some coffee. Over coffee he asked me what the job was, and so I told him I needed a survey map of a piece of land I wanted to buy. He told me he was a master surveyor and had worked on the rail road up north as a surveyor but now he had a ranch east of town. He asked me where the land was I wanted mapped.

"It's a day's ride west of town. It's a real large piece of land."

"I'll need some help on this job," he said. "I've got a trusty friend who's helped me in the past."

"What's that going to cost me?"

He thought about it for a minute, and then said it would cost me two dollars a day each, plus food. I told him that would be all right and when could he start.

"It'll take a week to make arrangements for me to be away from my ranch."

And so we shook hands and he left.

I walked over to the mercantile store and ordered a tent for the surveyors to sleep in and extra blankets, because it was still cold at night. And then I walked over to the livery to talk to George about a second pack horse. He was not there, and so I walked back to Polly's and found George sitting at the kitchen table drinking coffee. He was all shined up and smiled as I came in. He looked so different with his hair cut and slicked back. Polly told me he was staying for supper. I could see a love affair in progress and was pleased for them. After supper I left them alone and went for a long walk around town. That place felt like home to me. The next morning after breakfast I went to the livery to talk to George about a second pack horse, and he said he would get me one. I told him about the surveyors I had hired to map the valley, and he said if I needed help, to call on him. I thanked him and walked over to the mercantile with a list of supplies I would need for three weeks and three bags of oats for the horses, and so by the end of the week I had two good loads for the pack horses. The pack horse George had found for me was a little frisky, but I knew that by the time we got out to the valley he would calm down. Right on time, John Brower and his helper came into town with a pack horse loaded with surveying equipment, then with the three pack horses we left town. It took us a long day to get to the valley. John's helper James was a quiet man and only spoke when spoken to, but was good with horse, and so while he tended to the horses, John and I put up the tents, and I cooked a little supper. Then we went to sleep. In the morning while we were eating our breakfast, John asked me how much of the valley I wanted mapped.

I said: "All you can see inside the mountains, that includes the pond at the bottom of the valley."

They looked at each other and James said, "Holy Cow," and looked at me and smiled.

"That's a whole lot of land," John said. "It'll take some time to map."

I told them I would pay them a twenty dollar bonus if they could have it done in two weeks and I asked if I could help them.

"You do the cooking, that'll be help enough." Each night when they came into camp they would show me how much they had mapped that day. I could see they were covering a lot of ground. Each after noon I would go to the stream and pan for gold. By the end of two weeks I had another cloth coffee bag full of gold.

One night after supper John said there was a lot of timber in the valley and, with rumours of a railroad coming through Hope one day, the town could use all the lumber it could get. I gave it a lot of thought and told myself to look into it. By the end of the second week they had finished mapping the valley. I looked at the survey map, and then shook each man's hand and thanked them for a job well done. We left the valley on Saturday morning and arrived back in Hope late in the day. I got them rooms in the hotel, and then I paid them and gave them the twenty dollars bonus each I had promised and shook their hands. John told me if I needed help down the road to call him and James said, " It was nice meeting me." Those were the most words he had spoken in two weeks.

After a good night's sleep and a bath and haircut I went to see Bob at the bank and showed him the survey map of the valley. He looked at it for a long time then said it was a lot of land and he liked it. He added up the areas and said it was close to 6300 square acres. He told me he did not know how much property was going for, but the bank would help me buy it. Then he asked one of his clerks to make a copy of the survey map to keep in the bank. He also told me to have the mineral and timber rights put in the property deed. I thanked him and shook his hand and left the bank.

Chapter 9

The Clerk

WITH THE SURVEY MAP IN MY POCKET I RODE OVER TO county seat in Artesia to buy my valley. I tied my horse to the hitching rail in front of the town hall and went in and asked a lady behind the counter if she was the person I talked to about buying land. She said I had to talk to the county clerk and pointed to a stout lady talking to a co-worker, and so I went over to her counter and waited. She looked at me, then continued to talk to her co-worker. I stood there for a long while, trying to get her attention, but she still ignored me, and so I looked around and saw a man sitting at a desk in a back room. I went over and knocked on his door frame.

He looked up. "Can I help you? "

"I'm here to buy some land."

He told me to see the clerk at the front counter, I told him I had waited a long time for her, but she did not have any time for me given she was talking to her co-worker. He asked me about the land I was interested in.

"West of Hope. 6300 acres."

He got up and came around his desk and told me he was counselor Jackson. I told him my name and shook his hand. Then he walked over to the clerk's counter and waited. After a few minutes, the lady the clerk was talking to looked up and saw us standing there and turned and walked back to her desk. The clerk slowly turned around and looked at us. Mr. Jackson waited until she came over to the counter, then he told her I was Kaleb Jakobs and she had better treat me with some respect or she could go home and stay there. Her face turned blood red, In a sweet voice you would use on a child, she asked me what she could do for me. Mr. Jackson looked mad at her but said nothing, and so I told her I had come to buy a piece of land. She looked at me with a smug look on her face, and told me I had to have a survey map of the land I wanted to buy, then added it had to be done by a registered surveyor. I took the survey map out of my pocket and handed it to her and said it was done by John Brower a registered surveyor.

She looked at the map for a long time. "Sir, you must be crazy."

I took the map out of her hand and turned to Mr. Jackson and asked him if there was some place else in town I could go to buy the land. He took the map and asked me if I had seen the land firsthand, and so I told him I had helped do the survey and knew the land well.

Mr. Jackson turned to his clerk and told her that if she was not his sister-in-law he would fire her. "No more smart talk. You look after young Kaleb here."

After two hours of looking through deed books and records, the clerk told me the land I wanted was free and clear, and that I could buy it. She told me that land in that area was going for one dollar and twenty five cents an acre, but because it was over five thousand acres the price would be one dollar an acre plus twenty five dollars to register the land deed, for a total of $6325 dollars. I told her that was okay. "And, if you please, I'd like you to make out the deed to include the mineral and timber rights."

She looked at me with that smug look of hers and said she would have to have payment in full before she could register the deed, so I took out my cheque book and wrote a cheque for the full amount and handed it to her. She looked at the cheque, and then laughed at me and asked me what I thought I was doing and crumpled the cheque up and tossed it in the trash can. I could not believe what she had done, and so I called Mr. Jackson over and told him what she had done with my cheque. He went over and picked the cheque out of the trash can and straightened it out and looked at it. "Why the devil, did you throw his cheque in the trash!"

She had that smug look on her face again.. "Look at him. It can't be any good coming from a kid as young as him."

I asked Mr. Jackson to take the cheque to the bank, and so he asked me to go with him. On the way out the door, he stopped and told the clerk to have two copies of the deed ready when we got back from the bank.

At the bank Mr. Jackson gave my cheque to the bank manager, who sent a telegraph wire to the bank in Hope. In a few minutes, Bob wired back saying the cheque was good, and so Mr. Jackson asked me if I would like to have lunch with him for all the trouble his clerk had caused me. I told him I would like to eat at the hotel, because I liked the China lady's food. He smiled and said he liked it, too. At lunch I told him about the valley and how beautiful I thought it was.

"I'm pleased for you. I hope you make a good life for yourself out there."

After lunch we walked back to his office, and he asked his clerk for my deeds. She looked at him and said she had not done them.

"Why not?" he asked her scowling.

"Like I said, that cheque is surely no good, and I don't want to waste my precious time doing it."

Mr. Jackson called a clerk from the back and asked if she knew how to write up a deed She said she could, and so he turned to his sister-in-law and told her to go home and find another job. She did not work for him anymore. She left in a huff and slammed the door on her way out.

Mr. Jackson said he was sorry for the way I had been treated and said it would not happen again. He told me it would take some time for the new clerk to make out two copies of the deed with the mineral and timber rights, and asked if I would like to wait in his office and have some hot coffee. For the next hour I sat and listened to Mr. Jackson tell me about the plans he had for the county. When my deed was ready, Mr. Jackson signed it and handed it to me, and then shook my hand. "It was a pleasure meeting you. I'd be pleased if you would drop by any time you're in town."

So with the deed to my valley in my pocket, and a heart I thought would break with pride in m chest, I took my horse over to the livery stable, and then I walked over to the hotel and got the best room in the hotel for a dollar and had the China lady cook me a good supper. The next day I left Artesia after breakfast and got back to Hope in time to have supper with George and Polly. I told them about my problems over at the county seat, and then I went to bed. After breakfast the next morning I went to the bank and took five thousand dollars out of my valise and gave it to bob..the next day i found bob standing in frount of the bank with a worried look on his face. I asked him what was bothering him. He told me his daughter Jean had been in Dallas going to school and was on her way home. She was traveling by wagon train to Carlsbad then by stage coach to Hope, and she was late. I told him I had made the same trip and wagon trains were always late. He smiled at me and asked me to come into the bank. We went into his office and he asked a clerk to bring us hot coffee. i told him about the problems I had getting my valley registered. He asked me to come to supper when his daughter Jean finally got home, and I said I would. I shook his hand and walked over to the livery stable to talk to George and found him out back in the corral looking at a pair of young horses. He told me a rancher east of Hope wanted him to sell them for him. I asked George if they could be trained to pull a wagon. He looked at me with a smile on his face and said, "Yes, I should think so."

I told him I had bought the valley and would need a good, strong wagon and a team of horses to pull it to take supplies out to the valley. A price was agreed to and we shook hands and he said he was proud of me. We talked for a few minutes, and then I left and walked over to the mercantile store and went in and found the owner and told him my name. He told me he was Sol short for Solomon Rothberg and we shook hands. "I've seen you here in the store a few time. What can I do for you today?" Then he said he had heard that I bought a large piece of land west of town and smiled at me. "News travels fast in Hope."

I talked to him about some of the plans I had for my valley and asked him if I could get some lumber. He laughed. "All the lumber comes by wagon train from Hobbs, New Mexico and it can take months if it comes at all." He then told me if we had a saw mill in this area we could sell every board we could cut.

"How can I get a saw mill i aked him?"

He said he would look for one and let me know. Then he smiled and said it would be a good investment for a young man with lots of timber. As I walked back to Polly's, I thought that with a railroad coming to Hope some day I could make a lot of money.

Five days later, Sol sent a boy to find me. So I went to his store. He told me he had found a new sawmill, and it was in Amarello, Texas, and they wanted four thousand dollars for it. They would ship it to Hope for five hundred dollars more, and they would send two men to set it up and show us how to use it. I had Sol send them a wire saying I would buy it, and when could they have it in Hope. They wired back, asking me to put the money in the bank in Hope, and they would ship it, and we should have it in about six weeks. Sol and I went into his office for coffee. He asked me if he could be my lumber agent in Hope. I told him he could and shook hands on it. That afternoon I took six thousand dollars out of my valise and went to the bank and told Bob I had bought a sawmill for 4500 dollars, and could he put it in a special account for the man who was bringing the sawmill, and put an extra fifteen hundred dollars in my chequing account. Bob told me he liked the idea of having a lumber mill in the area. Two days later, while I was having coffee with Polly, a young boy delivered a note from Bob saying his daughter Jean had arrived home, and could I come to supper this evening. I wrote a note saying I would be pleased to come to supper and gave the boy ten cents and told him to take the note to Mr. Nelson at the bank. After coffee with Polly, I walked over to the livery and spent the morning with George and my horses. I now had five of them. George had started training the two young horses to pull the wagon he had found for me, and they were coming along just fine, and I was pleased.

Chapter 10

Jean

AFTER LUNCH I WENT TO THE BATH HOUSE FOR A BATH A haircut and a shave, then on to the mercantile store for some new clothes and coffee with Sol. At supper time I knocked at the side door of Bob's house. The door opened, and the most beautiful woman I had ever seen asked me if I was Kaleb Jakobs. I could not find my voice, and so I nodded yes and stepped in, and she smiled at me and took my hat. She told me she was Jean Nelson and held out her hand. I took it in mine and told her I was pleased to meet her. Her hand felt soft and so good, and she did not pull her hand away, and so we stood there until Bob came into the kitchen, and then I let her hand go. She smiled at me and the whole room lit up like a sun rise on a spring day. Jean left the room to help their housekeeper with supper, and Bob shook my hand and told me from now on I was to come to the front door. then he showed me to the parlour, and we sat down.

He asked me if I would like a drink. I said, "No, thank you," so he poured himself one and asked me about my plans for the sawmill. I told him half my valley was covered with good timbre and would make excellent lumber.

Just then Jean came in and told us supper was ready, so we followed her into the dinning room and sat down. While we were eating, Bob told Jean that I had bought a very large tract of land west of town. He said how this land was covered with timber, and how I had ordered a sawmill and was going into the lumber business and hoped to supply the whole area with lumber. Jean told us about her trip from Dallas. I told her I had made the same trip. She said she would not do it again and we laughed.

After supper, Jean and I sat on the front porch and Jean told me she had lost her mother when she was ten years old and said her father had done a good job of being mother and father to her. We talked until it got dark, and then we agreed to meet for lunch the next day at the hotel. I took her hand in mine and said good night and left.

I was feeling very good as I walked down Main Street when a big man came up to me and asked me if I was Kaleb Jakobs, I said I was. The next moment I felt a sharp pain on the side of my head and I fell to the ground. I felt his big boot as he stomped on me. The pain was unbearable. I felt my ribs break. He stomped on my left hand. And then everything went black.   When I woke up the big man was on the ground and George was sitting on top of him smashing his fists into the big man's face. I made a loud noise. George looked up, and then hit him on the nose with a devastating punch, and then got up and came

over to me and held my head in his hands and told me I was
going to be all right and ran off to get help.

A few minutes later he came back with the doctor and
the sheriff and some men to help. The sheriff put handcuffs
on the big man and had two men take him to the jail house.
The doctor looked at me and told George I was in very
bad shape, and he was to take me over to his office, and so
George left and came back with a wheelbarrow. They gently
lifted me onto it and wheeled me over to the doctor's office.
The pain was so bad I thought I was going to die. When we
got to the doctor's office, he mixed a powder in a glass of
water and had me drink it and said it would help with the
pain. Then he looked at my head and said he would have
to put some stitches in it and it would hurt a little, and it
did hurt. He straightened my nose, and I screamed in pain
and started to cry. About this time, Bob and Jean came
in to see what had happened to me. The doctor told them
I had received a bad beating and had some broken ribs and
a bad left hand, but that he did not think any of my fingers
were broken. He put another powder in a glass of water
and helped me drink it, saying it would put me to sleep so
that he could set my ribs. The last thing I remembered was
Jean holding my good hand.

The next morning I woke up in so much pain. I tried to
get up. The pain brought tears to my eyes and I lay back
down. In a short time, the doctor came in and gave me
another powder and said I needed more sleep. When I woke
up this time it was late the next day, and I felt a little better.
The doctor said that Jean had been by several times to see
how I was doing. That made me feel a lot better. At supper
time, Jean and Bob and George came by to see me and

Jean had made some soup, and George told me the man that did this to me was in jail and was not doing so well. I could smell the soup. I told Jean that I was very hungry. While she fed me the soup, George told us that he had seen the whole thing and was sorry he had not got there faster. I thanked him for saving my life, and that I would never forget it. He smiled at me and said it was no trouble at all. Bob and George left, and Jean finished feeding me the soup. She held my right hand and asked me how bad was my left hand,

"It hurts real bad, but it'll get better with more of your fine chicken soup."

She laughed. "Well, you do look a sight what with your head bandaged and your hand and ribs all wrapped in tape and your nose twice its normal size. Don't worry though, you're still handsome as the daylights."

Then she kissed me on my cheek and left. the next morning the sheriff came by to see me and asked me what had happend. I told him what i knew

. and said I did not know the man who beat me or why. He told me the man was in bad shape with a broken jaw and a smashed nose and that his eyes were swollen shut and he was not talking. The sheriff said he did not know what to do with him. I told him I would like to talk to him. He said he would bring him over as soon as he could.

Two days later, after a lot of Jean's chicken soup, I was able to sit up with not too much pain when the sheriff along with George brought the big man in and sat him down in a chair beside the my bed. I looked at him and saw that he was in as bad a shape as I was. His nose and jaw were swollen out of shape, and his eyes were swollen shut and several teeth were missing, and his face was criss-crossed with stitches.

"Could you be so kind as to remove the handcuffs," I asked the sheriff.

He did so reluctantly. The man rubbed his wrists and nodded to me.

"What's your name, then," I asked him.

He winced in pain. "Fred Jackson."

"Why-ever would you do this to me?"

"On account you disrespected my wife."

"Who might your wife be?"

"She's the county clerk over in Artesia."

I looked at him for a long minute. "I reckon I am the reason she lost her job, but I suggest you better talk to your brother about this before you do this to someone else who just might kill you. Any case, your wife ain't telling you the truth." I told him what really happened and said his brother would back up my story.

"Look, here," he sighed, "Hearing all that, I'll admit I'm sorry for the pain I caused you."

George took him out of the room, and I asked the sheriff what he was going to do with him. He said he was going to keep him in jail until the judge came to town and that he would let him deal with him.

That afternoon Bob and Jean came by to ask me if I would like to stay with them while I got better, and Bob said that way Jean and Saddy their house keeper could look after me better, and I would be on my feet in no time. I told them I would like that, and so Bob sent for George to help me over to their house and set me up in a room off the kitchen. George went over to Polly's house and packed up my belongings and brought them to Bob's house. He then told me he was moving in with Polly, because he was spending all his spare time there and was going to ask Polly to marry him. I smiled at him and said it was a great idea and that I was happy for him. So for the next month Jean and Saddy fussed over me, and I healed up real fast. One day I was sitting on the porch soaking up the sun when George came up the walk with a young man and sat down. The young man said he was Roy Mantle and held out his hand, and so I told him my name and shook it. I asked Roy where he was from, and he said Georgia, and he had lost his mother and father to the fever back in Fort Worth Texas and had worked his way over to Hope. He told me he was nineteen years old and had worked on the family farm until his father got into trouble because he did not believe in slavery, and so he decided to come west to find a better place to live. George said Roy had asked him for a job, and thought I might be able to use him when I got my sawmill. I told him the sawmill would be here any day now, and I could use him, and so George said he would look after him until I needed him. Over the next two weeks I got a lot stronger, and the doctor said I could go back to work, but to take it easy. I started to make plans to go out to the valley and sent word to the livery stable that I needed Roy and told him I was taking him with me to do the heavy lifting, and now that he was working for me I would get him a room at Polly's rooming house. He thanked me, and said it would be better than sleeping in the livery. That afternoon I took Roy over to the mercantile store to get the gear he would need when we started work in the valley. As the weeks went by, Jean and I became very close and would sit on the front porch each night after supper talking about what we wanted to do with our life, and Jean was teaching me mathematics and how to write a business letter so when the time came for me to start running the sawmill I would know how. Jean was now working for her father at the bank and liked it. One evening Roy and I were sitting at the kitchen table making plans to go out to the valley when Jean asked if she could come with us, and I said yes. She went and told Bob about her plan to go with us, and he told me to take good care of her, and I said I would. The next day Roy and I went to the mercantile store, and I gave Roy a list of supplies we would need, and I went to talk to Sol and asked him when he thought my sawmill would be here. He thought about it for a minute, and said it should be here any day now. Then we walked over to see George, and I told him I would need the wagon to take supplies out to the valley. He said he would have it ready when we needed it. Two days later, Jean, Roy and I went out to the valley. When Jean saw it for the first time her face lit up, and she said it was so beautiful. Roy and I put up two tents, one for Jean, and one for us, and while we made up the campsite Jean took my horse and went for a short ride and came back with a smile on her face and told us it was truly the most beautiful place on Earth. I put Roy to work getting fire wood while I helped Jean cook supper. After supper I showed her a place I thought would be a good place to build a house. She walked around the area, and then stopped in the middle and said it was the right place. I walked over to her and took her in my arms and said I loved her very much and kissed her. She told me that she had loved me from the first day she set eyes on me, and then she kissed me, and I kissed her back.

"Marry me," I said. And she said yes. I picked her up in my arms and danced around until I was out of breath, and then kissed her again. We went to tell Roy. He told us he was happy for us.

The next morning we staked out our house and Roy found a good place for a barn and a bunkhouse. Every chance I got I would kiss Jean, and Roy would laugh. By the end of the week we had the house, barn, and bunkhouse staked out and had found two good places to set up the sawmill. So we packed up our gear and went back to town. The next morning at breakfast I told Bob I had asked Jean to marry me and that she had said yes. He got up from the table and came around to slap me on the back, and said he was pleased. Then he kissed Jean on the cheek and told her he was proud of her.

Chapter 11

Weddings

THE NEXT MORNING AFTER JEAN AND BOB WENT TO WORK at the bank, I got out the coffee bag of gold that I had panned, and I took it over to the bank and asked Bob if he had a minute.

He laughed and said, "I always have time for you, Kaleb." And he showed me into his office. Once inside I put the bag of gold on his desk and told him I had panned it out of the stream in my valley. He got out a scale and put my gold on it and added weights to it and told me I had twenty ounces and that gold was going for twenty dollars an ounce. So that means it came to four hundred dollars. I looked at him and laughed, and then I shook his hand. He told me to bring all the gold I could find, and we all would be rich. I asked Bob to put the money from the gold into an account in Jean's name and not to tell her. He smiled at me and said he would.

The next Saturday afternoon George married Polly. It was the first big wedding in town. Everyone showed up. I stood up with George. And a close friend of Polly's stood up with her. To every one's surprise, Polly had asked Sol to give her away. He looked so proud as he walked her down the aisle. That evening they held a dance in the street. Jean and I danced most of them. I had a dance with Polly, and Jean had a dance with George and her father. When there was a break in the dancing, Bob got up and told everyone that we were going to be married soon, and everyone shouted that they were happy for us and there was lots of back slapping and kissing and stops at the punch bowel. Later in the evening I got very dizzy and walked into a wall and fell down. Some of the men carried me over to the doctor's office for some stiches over my left eye and, with lots of laughter, carried me home and put me to bed. In the morning I woke up with a bad headache and a black eye. I asked Jean what had happened. She laughed and said someone had put some home-made liquor in the punch bowel, and that I had gotten quite drunk. I told her I did not like what liquor did to me and that I would never drink it again. And I never did. After breakfast of toast and lots of strong black coffee I went to see George at the livery. On the way, the men in town slapped me on the back in fun and the women giggled as I walked by. George told me he was taking Polly to Carlsbad for a short honeymoon and would be back in about five days.

When they got back from their honeymoon, Jean and Polly spent the next two weeks planning our wedding and, on a warm clear Saturday afternoon, the town was treated to another big wedding. George stood up with me, and Polly stood up with Jean. And Bob, with the biggest smile on his face, gave the bride away. We had invited every one in town to the dance and everyone came and had a good time. Jean and I danced the first dance, then spent the rest of the evening dancing with our guests. This time I stayed away from the punch bowel. Polly made a beautiful big wedding cake, and there was not a crumb left by the end of the night. I was so happy. I told Jean she looked so beautiful in her wedding dress and that I loved her so much and I could not stop kissing her. We went out to our valley for a weeks honeymoon and spent most of it in our tent. But I found sometime to show Jean where I had found the gold and showed her how to pan. We got very wet, and she found a gold nugget and started to jump up and down, and so I grabbed her, and we both fell into the water laughing. We walked back to our campsite and took off our wet clothes and dried off by the fire, not feeling a bit ashamed of our nakedness and Life was good.

Chapter 12

The Sawmill

WHEN WE GOT BACK TO TOWN, BOB TOLD US THE SAWMILL had arrived. He had put the men who delivered it up at the hotel. The sawmill and horses were over at the livery stable. I thanked him and went looking for the men and found them in the hotel having lunch There were eight wagon drivers as well as the two men who had come to set up the sawmill and show us how to run it. I talked to them about their trip to Hope, and said I would send Roy Mantle with them to show the two places I had picked for them to set up the sawmill and for them to pick the best place. Then I went to see George about finding eight to ten men to cut down trees. He told me to put up a notice for help at the town hall. In the morning a group of men were waiting for me at the livery stable. I told them my name, and said I would talk to each of them first. I told them the work was a day's ride west of town, and it was full-time, and that I paid a dollar a day and all the food they could eat, and that they would have a dry place to sleep, a tent at first and then bunk houses.

Three men got up and went out, and so I talked to each of the men left and found that five of them had cut trees before and were called lumberjacks, and one had been a cook in the army, and so I hired him . Then I talked to the two men left. I liked them right off, and so I told them I would have them learn how to run the saw mill, and they liked the idea. Then one of them said he had a kid brother that he was responsible for and could he come with them. I asked him where he was now, and he said he was outside waiting, and so I told him to bring him in. The kid was tall for his age and looked like he had done some hard work. I asked him how old he was and what was his name. He told me he was twelve years old and that his name was Frank Skrens. The two men I had picked to run the sawmill were John Brown and Boris Skrens. I took them all over to Sol's mercantile store for the supplies they would need when they started work out in the valley, and I told the cook to order the supplies he would need including pots and pans and dishes and cups. The next morning we left town with our wagon full of supplies and men. Three of the men had horses to ride. Jean and I had our horses. And the two men sat on the tail gate of the wagon. Young Frank sat on top of the supplies with a big smile on his face. When we got close to the valley, Jean and I rode ahead to cook a meal for them when they arrived. The trip was uneventful. Roy and his gang had put up the tents for us, and so after supper everyone went to bed.

—◦———◦◦◦———◦—

In the morning Jean, with the help of the sawmill cook and young Frank to get firewood, made us a great breakfast with lots of hot coffee. Roy and his men had unloaded the sawmill, witch included a steam boiler, and they had it almost ready to go, and so I took the lumberjacks out to a place I thought would be a good place to start cutting timber so they would have a stockpile of logs ready when the sawmill needed them. One of the lumberjacks asked me if I had made any plans to replant the cut-out area. I told him I did not know about replanting, and so he said he would show me how. Then I took John and Boris and young Frank over to the sawmill and told the man in charge of setting up the sawmill to teach them how to run it. He said he could use young Frank to keep the fire going in the steam plant. Late in the afternoon they had the sawmill ready to go, and young Frank had built up a head of steam. They asked young Frank to pull the lever that started the sawmill running and, with a rush of steam, the saw blade started to turn. They spent the rest of the day making adjustments to the mill table, and said it would be ready to cut the first board in the morning.

The next morning young Frank had built up a head of steam, and we all watched as they rolled the first log on to the table and started it moving towards the spinning saw blade. When the log reached the blade, the noise was so loud we had to put our hands over our ears. The man in charge said we would get used to the noise, and we did. I was impressed as the first board came off.. and Jean said she would like to keep it and would put it on the wall of our house when it was built, and so I told Boris to put it in a safe place. He said he would. Then I shook hands with everyone and told them I was pleased.

That afternoon Jean and I went to our private bath place in the stream that was surrounded by trees and played in the water. Jean and I kissed and made love, and when we came to the camp everyone smiled but said nothing. After supper I asked the lead man what he was going to do with the wagons and teams of horses he had used to bring our sawmill. He said he had to sell them and use the money to get them home. I asked him what he wanted for them, and thought his price was a fair one, and so I bought them, and now I had the wagons to take my lumber to Hope. I put Roy in charge of the horses, and he told me he would need some fencing to keep the horses from wandering away. I agreed with him and said I would get some the next time I went to town.

We ran the sawmill for a week and had our problems. John and Boris, along with the two men that came with the sawmill, finally got it working right, and so I took the men that had brought the sawmill from Amarelo, Texas to town and put them up in the hotel. Then I took the lead man to the bank for his money. He thanked me and shook my hand and said it was a pleasure meeting me and wished me good luck with my sawmill. I went and stopped at Bob's house. In the morning I went to see Sol and ordered some fencing. He told me he had some out back and would order more. I told him we now had eighteen wagon horses and six riding horses, and I did not want them to wander off. I asked him if he could get me some strong chains to use for dragging logs to the sawmill. He said he would find me some. He asked me how the sawmill was doing, and so I told him he would have some lumber soon, and he was happy.

Roy had stayed in the valley and was in charge, and so when George and Polly came by and asked us to go with them to Carlsbad for a short holiday and to do some shopping. Jean said she would love to go. And so we went to Carlsbad where Polly helped Jean pick out furniture for our soon-to-be built home. We slept in each day and had late breakfasts with George and Polly, and then the girls spent the rest of the day looking in shops, and George and I looked at horses, saddles, and riding gear. On the second day George found a blacksmith that said he would move to Hope if we could help him find a shop. I told him I would help him and told him my name. He said he was Tom Smith, and he shook our hands. I said I would let him know when I had a shop for him. It was a nice few days off, and the last one we would have in a very long time.

When we got back to Hope I went looking for a shop for the blacksmith and found a burnt out building off Main Street and went and asked the town clerk about the property. She looked in her books and said I could have it for the taxes owing on it, plus ten dollars to change the deed. I asked her how much it would cost me to buy the place. She told me the price would be 160 dollars and the papers would be ready the next day. So I went looking for a carpenter and found two of them to change the burnt-out building into a blacksmith shop. They looked at the mess and said it would take at least a month to do. We agreed to a price, and they said they would start right away. After that I sent a note to Tom telling him I had a shop for him, and it would be ready in a months time. That evening after supper I asked Jean to join me on the porch and that I had something to tell her. She looked at me with a question on her face, so I told her about the money I had been given by Mrs. Roman and that I still had about 75,000 dollars—some of it already in the bank; some in a cloth valise in the safe at Bob`s bank. I told her I owned a one hundred acre farm in Hebron just outside of Chicago Illinois that was being run by my lawyer and a half interest in a large ranch just outside of Dallas Texas run by Alice and Jim Todd. I told her I had carried the money halfway across the country and no one knew about it. Jean looked at me with disappointment on the face, and I knew she was angry with me.

Finally she said, "No more secrets."

"No more secrets ever, I promise." And then I told her I had been putting the money in the bank a little at a time, but I had most of it in a valise in Bob's safe at the bank. I told her we could go to the bank and put the rest of the money in our account. She smiled at me, and said we should keep some out for emergencies. Then she asked me about the farm, and so I told her the whole story about why I had run away when I was twelve and my seven-year journey to Hope. I told her I had lived on the Devon ranch for just over two years to help them rebuild it and had bought half of it, and the profits I would receive from the ranch was to be put back to make the ranch bigger, and then I told her about the wagon train trip to Carlsbad and about meeting my cousin on the way. She looked at me with a smile and said she had married a rich man. I told her I had not earned the money and was using it to help people make their lives a little better.

————°○°————

The next morning we went to the bank, and I asked for my valise that Bob had been keeping for me in his safe. He brought it out and put it on his desk, and I opened it and let Jean take the money out and put it on his desk in front of him. Bob looked at the money and almost had a heart attack. When he recovered, he asked us where the money had come from, and so I told him the story of Mrs. Roman giving me the money. Jean took five thousand dollars and gave it to me and told Bob to put the rest into our chequing account. Bob counted the money and told us it was 65,000 dollars. He got out his ledger and wrote the amount in it and said our balance was just over 80,000 dollars and added that with that much money we should own the bank. I told him he could look after people's money, and I would look after Jean and our valley. Now Bob treated me like a son.

Chapter 13

Holly

ONE NIGHT AFTER SUPPER, BOB TOLD US SOL HAD COME to the bank to see about a loan to make his store larger, and he thought it would be a good investment for us. So Jean and I went to see Sol, and I asked him what his plans were for his store. He said he wanted to make his store bigger because rumours had it that the railroad would be coming to Hope soon, and he wanted to be ready. Jean asked him how much it would cost to make the changes he wanted. He told us about two thousand dollars. Jean smiled at me, and then asked Sol how much he would take for a half interest in his store. Sol looked at us for a long minute, and then asked us to step into his office for coffee and cake. After a lot of thought, he told us a half interest in his store would cost us eight thousand dollars. I looked at Jean, and she smiled at me and told me to write him a cheque. I did and handed it to him. He looked at the cheque for a minute, and then he put his arms around us. A tear ran down his face and he told us he was happy to have us as his partners, and then he took us to lunch at the hotel, and said he would have the papers ready for us to sign the next day. Then he shook my hand and kissed Jean on both cheeks. The next morning we met Sol at the town hall to sign the papers. We walked back to Sol's store and placed an order for supplies for the sawmill, and then went home for supper. Bob said we had made a good investment in the store, and said he was proud of us.

The next morning we took our supplies out to the valley. Roy was glad to see us and the rolls of fencing we had. It was late, and so we went to bed. In the morning we found a large pile of lumber and a second one growing beside it. Roy had been helping them drag logs to the sawmill, and Boris was teaching young Frank how to sharpen the spare blades so they could run all day. Then John told me they could use three more men to cut trees, and one to help at the sawmill. I told him I would find the men he needed the next time I went to town. John said he was pleased with the quality of the lumber they were cutting, and told me the lumber they cut with a sharp blade for the first hour was good for finishing work, and so he had put that lumber aside. I went and had a look at it. "You're right," I said.

The men had worked very hard, and so I thought it would be a good idea to take them all to town with the first loads of lumber, and so after a good breakfast we hooked up the horses to two wagons full of lumber and went to town. When we got there the people in town came out to see what was in our wagons, and so I told them they were looking at the first shipment of lumber from our sawmill and that they could buy some at Sol's mercantile store. I got rooms for everyone at the hotel and paid for their supper, and then Jean and I went to Bob's for the night. The next morning the lumber was all gone. I think Sol bought most of it to enlarge his store.

After breakfast we took the men over to Sol's store. He came out and shook each man's hand and patted young Frank on the head. I told Sol to give them what they needed to make life better out at the sawmill. So he took them in, and young Frank came running back out and asked Jean if he could have a coat he had found in the store, so we went in with him to see the coat and had him try it on. The red plaid coat was a little big for him, but Jean said he would grow into it. John said it would be a good idea to order more blades, so I asked Sol to order four new blades and Jean asked Sol to fill bags with penny candy for each man. Young Frank's bag was the fullest, and he had a big smile on his face and Boris asked Jean if he could trade his bag of candy for a box of cigars. She laughed, and said he could have both. We walked back to the hotel, the men with new hats, and young Frank with his new coat, and a large bag of penny candy. That afternoon I put out word that I needed help out at the sawmill. Then I went to see the finished blacksmith shop and found Tom and George standing in front of the shop with smiles on their faces. So I showed him the shop, and he said it was just right. So we came to a working agreement. He would work for me, and he would keep half of what he made, and my half would be put in a special account at the bank. Jean gave him his first job: to make a gate for the entrance to our valley, and she asked me if we could call our valley, Sun Valley Ranch.

I thought about it for a minute, and then said I loved it and gave her a big hug and a kiss. so now we had a name for our company that we would have to set up. I told Tom to make a sign for his shop saying it was the Sun Valley Blacksmith Shop, and I had opened an account over at the mercantile store for the supplies he would need.

The next morning, six men showed up at the livery stable. I had John and Boris talk to them and found out two of them were carpenters, and three of them were not wood cutters but lumberjacks, and one was a young man that would not make it out in the valley. So I told the first five men what I expected of them, and a wage was agreed to, and then I talked to the young man. He told me he needed a job because he had to support his sick mother, so I told him I had a job for him in town and then took the six of them over to Sol's store and told John to get them the gear they would need, and then I took the young man in to see Sol. I asked Sol if he could find some work for him. Sol said he would need help now that his store was going to be bigger. The young man thanked me, and then went to tell his mother. I told Sol I would need nails and hardware to use when I built my house and the bunk houses, and a standing order for food supplies to be picked up by the lumber wagon. He said he would have the order ready when the wagon came for it. So, with one wagon full of supplies, and the other wagon full of men, we went back to the valley. With the extra men at the sawmill we were now sending four loads of lumber a week to Hope, and the carpenters were taking lumber for the first bunkhouse they had started to build. Jean looked at the first building going up, and said she wished it was our house that was being built, and so I put my arms around her and kissed her. Then i told her the working men needed the first building and our house would not be far off, she smiled and said it would not be soon enough.

○———○○○———○

The next time Roy and I went to town, I went to see Bob at the bank. He suggested we form a company, and so I asked him to set it up, and said that the next time Jean and I came to town we would talk to him about it. While I was in the bank, Roy went over to see Tom at the blacksmith shop to have him make some hardware for the sawmill. When I finished at the bank I walked over to the livery stable to talk to George, there Roy found me. He had a young woman with him. He told me she had come off a wagon train and was looking for work and a place to live. I told her my name and she said she was Holly Bridger.

"Why did you leave the wagon train," I asked.

"You don't want to know," she said and frowned.

"What can you do?"

"I can cook and I've gone to school to be a dress maker and I'm not afraid of hard work."

Roy could not keep his eyes off her, and so I told her she would be a big help to my wife Jean and told Roy to take her over to Bob`s house for the night. In the morning we picked up our supplies and went back to the valley. Jean was glad for the extra help and took to Holly right away, and made her a bed in the kitchen tent. Every time I went by the kitchen tent I could hear laughter or the women were humming to themselves, and I knew Holly was good for Jean. The carpenters were now working on the second bunkhouse. When they finished it they had to build a proper cookhouse, and then they could start on our house. I was pleased about that. Every free minute Roy had we would find him at the kitchen tent. And in the evenings after supper we would see them sitting on a log at the stream holding hands with their heads together. Jean said it would not be long before something happened. She was right. Two weeks later, Roy and Holly came to us and said they would like to get married. I looked at Jean and we laughed.

Jean said, "What took you so long?"

And we hugged them, and told them we were pleased for them. That night at supper I told Roy to pick a place to build his house, and so they picked a place next to our house. I told the carpenters to build their house as soon as our house was finished. Jean and I and Roy and Holly went to town to make arrangements for their wedding and to buy things for our house. We were only in town for an hour when Roy came rushing up to us and told us the minister was leaving town. He would have to marry them before he left, or they would have to wait until he came back next month. Roy asked us to stand up with them. We said we would. Then Jean took Holly shopping for a dress while I went with Roy to buy some new clothes and a ring. We could not find a ring, and so I told Roy I had some nice rings I had gotten at Mrs. Romans' house. So Jean loaned Roy her ring, and Holly asked George to give her away. He was so pleased. Bob put on a great supper. Polly made a beautiful wedding cake. And the ladies in town brought lots of cold root beer. There was plenty of back slapping and kisses, with Roy doing most of the kissing. It was a good day.

The next day Jean and I talked to Bob about setting up a company. He said it was a good idea. Jean said she would like to call it the Sun Valley Holding Company, and we agreed, and so Bob said he would have the papers ready for us to sign the next time we came to town.

A month later Roy's house was finished and we started on the barn. We now had four men and young Frank working at the sawmill, as well as eight lumberjacks and six teamsters taking lumber to town. I made John foreman over the lumber operation and put Boris Skrens in charge of the sawmill. When the barn beams were ready to be put in place, I asked John to bring his men. Roy brought some horses to help put the beams in place. After the beams were up it took the carpenters three months to finish it. Then they built a bunkhouse beside the barn. When they finished all the work they could for the time being, I took everyone that worked for me to town. We had two wagons full of lumber and two wagons full of men. There was lots of laughter on the way to town. Jean and Holly joined in the fun, making it a good trip. When we got to town the men went to the bath house for baths and haircuts, and then on to the hotel for a late supper on me. It was quite a joyous affair.

———○○○———

I got rooms for them and told them to sleep in, and then Jean and I went to Bob's house. In the morning after a lazy breakfast we all walked over to Sol's store. He met us at the front door and shook hands with the men and made a big show of shaking young Frank's hand. This made Frank stand a little taller and everyone smiled. Then Sol invited them into his store to do their shopping and asked Jean and I to step into his office for coffee and cake. I knew he had something on his mind, and so I asked him. He said he would like to change the name of his store. Jean looked at me, and then asked him what name he had in mind. He told us he would like to call it the Sun Valley Mercantile Store. Jean thought about it for a minute, and then looked at me with a smile on her face.

"I like it," she said, and I agreed and shook Sol's hand.

○———○○○———○

After an hour of shopping, the men had what they needed, and so we walked back to the hotel, the men with new clothes and wearing new hats, and Boris with his box of cigars, and young Frank with a new coat because his plaid one was in bad shape. He carried, too, a large bag of penny candy.

By now the lumber mill was putting out a load a day, and so we sent two wagon loads every other day, which meant we had wagons coming and going *every* day. Roy told me some of the horses were getting tired, and he would like some young horses so the older horses could have a longer rest. Off we went to see George about getting us eight to ten more horses. He said he would get them for us, and that he would drive them out to the ranch for us. I thanked him and went to find Jean, who was talking to John in the hotel. He said he could use at least four more men, and so I went and found them for him and he said they would do just fine. Jean and I then went to see Bob at the bank. He smiled at us as we walked in, and asked us to join him in his office, and then asked one of his clerks to bring us coffee. Then he went over our accounts. He said the blacksmith shop was holding its own, and that the mercantile store was doing very well with the added sale of lumber. He noted that even with the large amount of wages we were paying out each month we were still making money. He told us that he had heard from a good source that the railroad would be coming through Hope, and that it would be a good idea to buy some property in town, and so Jean and I walked through town looking for property and found three good pieces of land on Main Street and two large pieces of land outside town that could be useful when the town got bigger. We went to see the town clerk and had her look up the property we wanted. She looked in her book and told us we could buy them for a good price of a thousand dollars for all five properties.

"We'll take them all," I said and wrote her a cheque.

She said the paper work would be ready by this afternoon.

"Register the properties in the name of the Sun Valley Holding Company."i said.

She said she would and would send them over to the hotel when they were ready. We thanked her and went back to the hotel. We stayed over that night and left town in the morning with our wagons loaded with supplies and men. I felt good. Sun Valley Holding Company. I could say it all day and night.

Chapter 14

Gems

ONE AFTERNOON WHEN EVERYONE WAS WORKING, I TOOK Jean to the place on the stream where we had panned for gold on our honeymoon. I got the pan I had hidden under some bushes and started to pan. Jean said she was going for a walk up the stream, and so I panned for about an hour. Then Jean came back with something bundled up in her skirts and showed me a colored stone. It looked nice, and so I took it and rubbed it on my shirt sleeve, and then licked it with my toung and rubbed It and it started to shine. Then I remembered seeing a picture just like it in the book George Brown had given me. I could not remember its name, but I knew it was a gem. Jean dumped the stones on the ground and told me there were dozens of them up where the stream came out of the rocks. She took my hand and we walked up to the place she had found the stones. There they were, strewn all over the ground. I picked up a stone that looked different and rubbed it on my pants. It came up a shining black.

"Let's take them back to the house," I told Jean. "And I'll look in my gem book." I tried to sound nonchalant, but my heart was beating with excitement.

Then we went back to the place I had been panning, and I showed her the gold I had found. She laughed and danced around me and said she loved me.

That evening after supper I got out my gem book. We looked through it until we found pictures of the stones Jean had found. The first one was a turquoise and the second was an opal. The other stones looked like jasper and agates. I told Jean I thought she had found a fortune in gem stones and gave her a big hug.

The next afternoon we went back to the stream. Jean carried a pail and a spade. She also carried a cloth coffee bag to put the gold in. We worked for two hours. Jean had filled her pail with stones; I half-filled my coffee bag with gold. We took the stones and gold to the house. With the gold I had already panned the coffee bag was almost full and quite heavy. I told Roy the next morning Jean and I were going to town and that he was in charge. When we got to town we went to see Bob at the bank and showed him the gold we had. He got out his scales and put the gold on it and told us it was thirty-two ounces and came 640 dollars and asked me if he should put it in Jean's account, then stopped and looked at me. I told Jean I had been putting the money I got for the gold into an account in her name. She looked at us and smiled and asked Bob how much was in her account.

He looked in his book and said. "You have eleven hundred dollars."

At that she hugged us both. "You're both so very bad, but in the best way." And we all laughed.

○────○○○────○

We stayed at Bob's house that night. The next morning we went to see Sol. He was glad to see us and was proud of the new sign hanging on the front of his store which read:

The Sun Valley Mercantile Store,
Owners Solomon Rothburg & Jean & Kaleb Jakobs

He looked so proud and Jean smiled at him and gave him a big hug. His store was now twice its original size and had so many supplies that they were stacked out front. He said business was good and that the young man I had brought him was now his assistant manager and was running half the store. Over coffee and cake, Sol told us lumber was being sold as fast as we could ship it, and he could sell a lot more if he had it.

"Sawmill's working as fast as it can, Sol," I told him

"Then maybe it's about time you bought another," Sol said.

"I guess I'll have to think about that."

Jean showed him one of our stones. He looked at it for a long time, and then said it needed to be polished.

"How do you go about polishing stones," I asked.

"Why, you'd need a gem polisher."

"Can you find us one?"

He said he would try. That evening we had supper with Polly and George and had a good visit with them.

We went to Bob's house for the night. After breakfast with Bob, we walked with him to the bank and spent the morning going over our accounts. When we were finished Bob told us we were getting rich fast. He said he was proud of us for what we had accomplished. A week later a note from Sol came out to us with a lumber wagon saying he had found a gem polisher that a man in St. Louis would sell us for five hundred dollars and that he would come and show us how to use it. I sent a note to Sol asking him to send a telegraph wire saying I would buy it. The man wired back saying he would need the fare for him and the gem polisher, and so I asked Sol to wire him the money he needed and to give him the directions to our valley.

Whenever Jean had some spare time she would take her pail and go pick stones. Now had a small pile of stones in the barn. My gem book told me if we found gem stones on the ground there would be a plenty more under it. I knew she would run out of stones on the ground soon, and we would have to start digging for them.

One day Jean took me to the barn and showed me the pile of stones she had picked up.

"We should have a place to hide them," she said. And so we looked around. "Why don't we dig a hole in the corner of the barn and hide them there," she suggested.

I agreed. I asked John for two men to dig the hidey hole and board it in with a ladder and a strong lid, but I told them it was for cold storage. When it was finished, we showed it to Roy and told him to keep it to himself. He thanked us for showing it to him and promised not to tell a living soul.

Winter was mild that year with only six weeks of bad weather, and it did not cause us much discomfort. The sawmill ran right through it. The demand for lumber was growing, and so I decided to order a new sawmill. I had a meeting with Roy and Jean and told them my plan. They thought it was time for a new and larger sawmill. John said we should move our sawmill to a new location and when the new one came we could set it up in an area with plenty of timber. John asked me if I had given any thought to replanting the cut-over areas.

"No, but I'll looking into it," I said.

It took us a week to move the sawmill and get it working again. I sent a note to Sol asking him to order a bigger sawmill and to let me know how he made out.

One evening Jean and I were sitting on our porch having coffee with Roy and Holly when a lumber wagon came up to the house with a passenger —a man in a suit.

"That must be the gem man with the polisher," I said.

When the wagon stopped in front of our house, the man got down and brushed the dust off his clothes and walked towards us, and so I went down to meet him.

He stopped and stared at me, and then smiled and said, "You are Kaleb Jakobs."

"And you're George Brown!"

We wrapped our arms around each other and slapped our backs and laughed. I took him up on the porch and introduced him to my wife Jean and to my best friend, Roy Mantle, and his wife, Holly. I told them we had traveled from Chicago to St. Louis on the train together and said it must be almost five years ago and shook their hands.

"Did you learn to read yet?"

"Yes, I have. And that gem book you gave me is one of my most treasured possessions and I've studied it so much it's nearly falling apart."

He smiled and said he had a new one for me, and I was pleased. I asked him where the gem polisher was. He said he had left it in Hope with the sheriff because he did not know what he would find when he got here. I told him it was a good idea and I would send a note with the next lumber wagon going to town to let the sheriff relese the gem polisher and let my lumber wagon bring it out to us.

✦

I asked him what he had been doing for the last five years. He said he had worked at a number of gold mines and that the last one closed down two weeks before we contacted him about his gem polisher.

That night Jean showed George one of her stones. He looked at it and rubbed it on his shirt sleeve, and then took out a small black case and opened it and took out a small file and hammer. He worked on the stone for a few minutes, and then told us it was a turquoise stone of very good quality and quite valuable.

Jean smiled at me. I knew she was thinking of the pile of stones we had in the barn. She gave him some more stones to look at. He told us one was an opal. One was a jasper. And that the large one was an agate. He added that there was a very good market for the gemstones we had found. He stayed with us for the night. After breakfast the next morning we moved him into the bunkhouse beside the barn. He said he would be very comfortable there. That afternoon, the polisher arrived on a lumber wagon. We needed Roy to help us get the wooden box up on our porch, and so Roy went and got a crowbar and opened it. Inside was the gem polisher. I thought it was beautiful. We took it out of the box. George attached the flywheel to the polisher drum and turned it with a hand crank. The polisher turned, and that made me happy. George said if we had power to drive it, it would be faster and easier than a hand crank as that would require a man turning it all day long.

Roy looked at the flywheel. "We might be able to hook it up to the drive wheel on the steam plant that runs the sawmill," he said, and so I sent for John.

He came and looked at it and said it might work. After two days of trying they made it work by running a smaller belt beside the main drive belt to the polisher that we had fastened to a solid wood platform; it started to turn the polisher, but George said it was turning too fast. So Roy took the flywheel into town and had Tom our blacksmith make a larger flywheel. When he put it on the drum, it turned it at the right speed, and so George went to the stream and got a pail of fine sand and told us to put a small amount of sand in the drum with the stones. "The sand will polish the stones," he said.

So Jean went and got a small pail of stones and George showed us how it was done. I had George train young Frank how to operate the polisher. He learned real fast and was soon putting sand in the polisher drum and keeping the fire going in the steam plant. It sure kept him busy. After they shut down the sawmill for the day, young Frank came to the house and showed us the first batch of stones he had polished. They looked beautiful. I thanked him and said I was proud of him, Frank smiled at us and went back to the sawmill.

I turned to Jean and smiled. "From now on, I think he should only be Frank. I don't want to hear any one call him young Frank, even though he's only thirteen."

She agreed with me, and then Jean picked a nice gemstone and said she would like to put it with the first board-cut and the first gold nugget she had found, and I thought it was a good idea, and then I hugged and kissed her and told her I loved her very much.

That evening I called a meeting with Jean and Roy and told them we would have to start digging for gemstones and asked them what they thought about asking George if he would like to work for us and if he did putting him in charge of digging for gemstones. They thought it was a good idea, and so the next morning I asked George if he would like to work for us. He said he would be pleased to, and so we took him to the place Jean had found the first gemstones. He looked around for a while and then told us there should be lots of gemstones in the ground where the stream came out of the mountain and with a lot of help he would find them. With the polisher working five days a week we soon had a large bag of polished turquoise and jasper and a few opals. We took them to town and showed them to Bob. He could not believe his eyes and told us they were beautiful. I asked him what we should do with them. He said he knew a man in New York City that might be able to sell them for us, and that he would send a telegraph wire to him and let us know. We spent the rest of the afternoon hiring two men to work with George at our new gem mine and sent them out on a lumber wagon with a note for Roy.

The very next day the man in New York City wired back, saying he was interested in what we had for sale and was sending one of his agents to see us. Bob thought it would take the agent about a month to get here, and that he would send word when he arrived. We went back to the valley and worked with George at his dig and was surprised that almost every shovelful of durt they dug out had a gemstone in it. Exactly a month later we got a note that the gem agent had arrived in Hope, and so Jean and I took our gems and went to town.

The agent told us that, with the railroad from New York City on to Dallas, Texas then west to Abelene and stage coaches to Hope, it only took him a month to get here. The agent brought us news that the north would go to war with the south soon, and it did not look good for any of us. Jean showed him our gemstones. He got out a magnifying glass and held it to his eye and looked at the stones for a long time, and then he told us they were a very high quality, and he could get us a very good price for them in New York and could sell all we could find. He told Bob to open a bank account in New York City because of the pending war. Jean and George came up with a clever plan to have Jean stich bags with numbers on them, and George would grade the stones and write the value he thought we should get for each stone so when they were shipped to New York we could keep track of them. We gave the agent four bags of gems to take back with him and thanked him for coming all this way and wished him a safe trip home and told him we would send more stones as soon as we could.

Chapter 15

War

I was wrong about the war coming to New Mexico, because that spring (1861) the South went to war with the North. Six months later small groups of men started leaving New Mexico to go to Texas to join up with the southern army. We were far enough away from the war, and our men did not want to go. The valley went on as usual. One day I spotted a covered wagon coming up the valley towards our house. I saw people walking beside it and went down to greet them. They were black people, and in bad shape. I called out to them and waved my hand. The driver waved back and pulled his wagon to a stop in front of our house. He jumped down and brushed the dust off his cloths. I went up to him and told him my name and held out my hand. He looked at my hand then looked at me and said his was Ezekiel Jones and shook my hand. Then he pointed at the women standing beside the wagon and told me they were his family. I asked him to bring them up on the porch and have a seat. The women stayed by the wagon, and so I told him to please bring his family up on to the porch. He called to them. A young boy with a rifle he could hardly lift stood up in the wagon. I told him he did not need the rifle in my valley and to come up for a cold drink, and so he jumped down and followed the women onto the porch. I asked Ezekiel where they had come from. He told me all the way from Monroe Louisiana and they were free slaves trying to get away from the war.

I told him I did not believe in slavery, and every one who worked for me got paid a fair wage. I asked him why he had come this way. He said he had stopped in Hope to get a wheel fixed, and the man at the livery stable said he might find work if he came to the Sun Valley Ranch and told him how to get here.

At this point, Jean came out to see what was going on. I told her George had sent them. She told them her name and shook their hands. I could see it was something they had never done with white people. Ezekiel pointed to his wife and said she was Mary, and her sisters were Dedria and Angel, and the young boy was their son Tomas. Jean asked them if they were hungry. They all nodded 'yes,' and so she asked the ladies if they would like to help make supper. So with smiles on their faces they followed Jean into the house. Ezekiel told me Tomas was ten years old and big for his age. In a few minutes, Mary came out with a tray with glasses and a large jug of root beer. Ezekiel said they did not drink spirits. I laughed and told him I did not allow spirits in my valley, and added that he would like root beer and that Tomas would like it the most. Ezekiel and I talked for a while, and then he asked if there was work for him out here. I told him I would find work for his whole family, even Tomas. I thought Tomas could take over Frank's job, and then Frank could help his brother on the sawmill. We had a good supper with everyone sitting at the same table. I had to tell them out here we are all equal, and it was all right for us to sit together. Tomas drank lots of root beer. After supper I showed Ezekiel a good place to park his wagon and told him to put his horses with our horses, and if he needed more tents I had them. I told him if he decided to stay and work for me I would build a house for them to live in. He came over to me and shook any hand and said God was smiling down on me today.

So Mary and Dedria went to work with Jean cooking, and Angel went to work with Holly repairing the men's clothing, and Roy took Ezekiel up to the gem mine to work with George, and Tomas took Frank's place looking after the fire in the steam plant and the gem polisher, and they became best of friends. The two carpenters were almost finished putting up Ezekiel's house, and so I went and asked them if they would like to put up shoring timbers in the gem mine, and they said they would. One day I was up at the mine and George told me they were finding small pockets of gold and showed me a pile of rocks with gold in them. He asked me if he could have two men to break the rock to get the gold out. So I asked the carpenters to build a cook house and add onto the bunk house and to build a cabin for George. I went to town and found two men to work at the mine and a cook, and so now we had ten men working at the mine. A few weeks later, Jean went up to the mine looking for me. George told her he had not seen me all day, but said he would tell him she was looking for him if he came by. She started down the trail, and then stopped. She had forgotten to invite him to Sunday supper and walked back to tell him. That's when she saw him go into his cabin with a large bag of gems, and so she went and looked in the window and saw him open a trapdoor in the floor under the table and put the bag in and close the door and pull the table back over it. Jean thought it was strange and hurried to find me and found me in the barn helping Roy fix a wagon wheel. She told us what she had seen. Roy and Jean and I walked up to the mine and found JOHN sitting on his porch, drinking coffee.

"How's it going, George ," I said, trying for calm.

"Everything's swell."

"Can I talk to you in your cabin?"

He looked at me, and then got up and we walked into the cabin.

"You got anything to tell me?" I asked.

He looked at us, and then stepped in front of the table but Roy pushed him aside, and I moved the table, and Jean showed me where she had seen john put the bag of gemstones.

I opened the trap door and saw there what looked like several bags of gemstones. At this point, George pushed past Roy and grabbed his gun and pointed it at me, his face red with fury.

"Everywhere I goddamn work. Everywhere! I make them rich.this time i am keeping what i find.

Jean gave me a look, and then pushed john as he pulled the trigger. The gun went off, and the bullet hit me in the arm. I grabbed the barrel of his gun and twisted it around.

He pulled the trigger again, and the bullet went in under his rib cage and came out at his neck. A shocked look came over this face, and then he fell to the floor, dead.

I sent a note to the sheriff saying we had a shooting and could he come. The next day he came and told us that as far as he was concerned it was self defence on my part. The next day we buried john . One of the carpenters made a marker and carved on it:

George Brown
Died of Misfortune. 1863

For the next two weeks Jean nursed my wounded arm, and Roy asked me if I thought it would be a good idea to put Ezekiel in charge of the mine and maybe Jean could teach him what to look for in my gem book.I thought it was a good idea, and so I asked Ezekiel if he would like to be the mine foreman. He said he would try to do a good job and thanked me for having faith in him. So Jean and Ezekiel would get together each night after supper on our porch and go through my gem book. Jean said he was a fast learner.

—o————oOo————o—

The next Sunday Jean asked everyone working on the ranch to supper. We had to put four tables together on our porch and Jean, with the help of Mary and her sisters, put on a great meal with lots of hot coffee and cold root beer. When we sat down, Roy put his arm around Holly and told us she was going to have a baby. We all were happy for them, and Mary told Angel to stay with Holly until the baby was born. So the women spent their spare time making baby clothes with lots of laughter. It was a grand time. Three months later, Jean told me I was going to be a father. I was so happy I picked her up and swung her around and around, and then stopped and put her down stricken.

"Have I hurt you? I hope not."

She laughed and said, "No, silly."

Holly had a girl. They named her Summer. Three months later we had a boy. We named him Tanner. The next year Holly had another girl. They called her Jenny. And we had a second boy and we called him Sander. Then we had a girl and we called her Amery.

That year the war raged back and forth, and New Mexico joined with Texas to form an army, and so groups of men went over to Texas for the second time to fight for the south. One day Ezekiel came to me and said he wanted to go north to join up. I told him he could go, but his family needed him, and I needed him. And then he said that his family had gone through too much already in their life, and so he said he would stay.

Jean and I wanted to help the south, and so we sent ten thousand dollars to General Lee in Columbus Georgia. Two months later we got a letter back fromGeneral Lee thanking us for our gift to his war effort. He said it helped him greatly, and he thanked us again and signed it *General Robert E. Lee*. Jean was so pleased that she put the letter with the first board we cut, and the first gold nugget and gem stone we found.

———∘○∘———

News of the war came slow to our valley, and it said the war was going badly for the south. Life, however, went on as usual throughout the war years, and we added a second sawmill that was bigger and could cut lumber faster. So now we had more wagons going to town every day. And we now had thirty men working for the Sun Valley Lumber company. John was their general foreman. Boris was running the new sawmill. Frank was running the old sawmill. Tomas looked after the gem polisher. Ezekiel had ten men working at the Sun Valley Mining Company. And Roy now had three cowboys working with the horses and ten teamsters. And so we now had fifty-six men and four women on our payroll. And everything was going better than I could have ever hoped for.

—○○—

Jean and I did not go to town much because our company was growing, and we needed to be there. The women were run off their feet looking after five little ones, all with wills of their own. I would look stern when one of them got into trouble and was sent to me for discipline. I would whisper in their ear and tell them to cry out when I paddled them lightly on their bum, and Jean would tell me I was spoiling them. And so I told her I would be firmer when the time came, and she would smile at me and take the disciplined one into the house.

Chapter 16

Rebels

ONE DAY A LONE RIDER CAME UP THE VALLEY TO OUR house. He looked in bad shape, and his confederate uniform was dirty and torn. He got off his horse and walked up to the porch and said his name was Billy Toms and he was from Little Rock Arkansas..

I told him my name and shook his hand.

"The war is over," he said. "The North won."

I asked Mary to bring something for him to eat and a jug of cold root beer. Billy said he did not drink spirits, and so I told him, like I told Ezekiel, that I did not allow spirits in my valley and asked if he would like root beer. He did.

"What are you going to do with your slaves?"

I looked at him for a minute. "What do you mean?"

"Slavery's been abolished. No one can own slaves anymore."

I laughed and said: "There's no slaves in my valley. Everyone in my valley gets paid."

"Huh. So how many people work for you?"

"Fifty to sixty at last count."

He looked around. "That's a lot."

While he was eating he told me about gangs of Northern and Southern rebels running wild, killing and robbing and burning ranches. He said we were far enough away they might not come, but he was not too sure. He asked me if there was work around here for a worn-out soldier. I said I could find work for him. I asked him what he did before the war. He told me had been a farmer, but his farm had been destroyed by the Northern army, and he no longer owned it. I asked him if he were good with horses. He said he was. I asked him if he would like a job looking after our horses. He smiled, and said he would and shook my hand. I told him to go over to the bunk house beside the barn and make himself at home.

That afternoon I called a meeting with Roy and Jean and told them I had hired a man to look after our horses and the cowboys that worked for Roy, and then I told Roy I was making him general foreman over the valley and said Ezekiel and John and Billy would report to him, and he and I would have regular meetings. He shook my hand and said he would do his best.   Our business was growing, and I had to spend more time in the office than I wanted to. On a rare trip to town Bob told us we had about ten thousand dollars of confederate money in his bank, and that it was no good. He said he knew we had large amounts of money in Chicago and New York banks, and I told him a lawyer by the name of Benjamin Goldstein was looking after them for us. Bob knew we had been sending money North all through the war, and so I told him we had close to 400, 000 dollars in our gem account in New York and, at last count, we had 150, 000 dollars in Chicago. Bob told us we had 175,000 in our chequing account, and about 75,000 dollars in gem stones, ready to be shipped to New York.

I told Bob to burn the confederate money, and he said he would. We stayed in town for two days to have a visit with Sol and George and Polly and a visit with Tom at our blacksmith shop, and then we went back to our valley. Life is funny sometimes, because a week later a note came from Bob telling us his bank had been held up by bank robbers. He had not yet burned the confederate money—it had been in bags by his desk— and so he gave it to the robbers. Off they rode out of town with bags of useless money with the sheriff shooting at them.

I showed the note to Jean, and we laughed.

◦——◦○◦——◦

One day, Jean and I were sitting on our porch having lunch when she looked around and said, "By the looks of things we're building our own town, because we now have three houses, a barn, and a bunk house, and two bunk houses at our sawmills, and a cook house and two bunk houses and another cook house and a foreman's cabin at our gem mine."

I had to agree with her. The next day the sheriff rode out to see us and was impressed at how the Sun Valley had grown. He told us a band of rebel Southern soldiers had been seen in the area, robbing and burning ranches and killing people. He told us they had attacked John Woods' ranch east of town and had killed him and his wife. His three kids had been at a neighbour's ranch for a birthday party and were now being looked after by that neighbour. I told the sheriff I would help them any way I could, and

I did. I had Bob open an account for them. Each month Bob would put one hundred dollars in it for them. The sheriff stayed the night. In the morning, before he left, he told us to keep a sharp eye out for them. That afternoon I called a meeting with everyone in the valley and told them what the sheriff had told me.

Roy said, "We should have a plan."

Billy Toms stepped forward. "I got fighting experience and I can help us."

"Then you're in in charge of defending the valley," I said.

The next morning, Billy took people that could not shoot a gun out in small groups and showed them how to shoot even better. Then he showed everyone where to go when the alarm was shouted. He asked me if we had any dynamite. Ezekiel said he had some up at the mine, and so I sent him and some of his men to get it and bring it to the barn. Meanwhile, Billy looked around and told me a rock outcrop about two hundred yards from the houses would be a good place for the rebels to hide when we started to shoot at them. He said if we buried the dynamite around the rock outcrop and ran the wicks to a spot behind a big rock off to one side, we might be able to blow them up before they could hurt us. I asked for a volunteer to light the wicks. Frank said he would, and so we buried the dynamite in a circle around the rock outcrop and ran the wicks to where Frank would be hiding. Then Billy showed each person that could shoot from the windows how he wanted them to aim their rifles, and what to shoot at, and to wait for my signal shot, and to fire their rifles as fast as they can until we told them to stop. Two days later Billy came riding as fast as he could up to the house. He told us he had seen a large group of rebel soldiers at the entrance to our valley, and so I sent him to get Ezekiel and his miners, and I went to get John and his men at the sawmill. When Billy got back, he told everyone to go to assigned place. "And you all wait for my signal shot," he said.

Frank went to his hiding place and waited.

•━━━━━○○○━━━━━•

As they came up the valley, I counted about fifty riders and two supply wagons coming in a close groups. They made great clouds of dust. It looked bad for us, but I had faith in my people, and so we watched them come up the valley. They were not in a hurry, and did not suspect us waiting for them. When they got even with the rock outcrop I fired my gun. At that, everyone opened fire on the rebels.

Five rebels in the front row went down. Our fire was so intense the rebels fell everywhere. The ones not shot ran behind the rocks and started to shoot back. We were shooting from the upstairs windows, and we were able to keep them pinned down behind the rocks, and so I waved to Frank. He lit the wicks and ran.

He got about ten feet and went down and I knew he had been shot. Then the first explosion happened. Bodies flew through the air. Then another explosions went off. Then another. When the smoke and dust cleared there was nothing left of the rocks, but bodies lay all over the place. Some of them moving and crying out for help. Billy went out first to check on Frank. He found him with a bullet hole in his shoulder and a bad cut on his head, but he was alive and would make it. Three of our men had been wounded. We found Ezekiel's sister-in-law dead with a bullet hole in her head. Five of the rebels were not badly hurt. The rest of the rebels died by sundown. We buried Angel beside john Brown. It was a sad time. Billy said we should take the dead rebels to town so other rebel groups would hear about what we did, and not come this way. So we loaded the dead in their two wagons and took them to town. By the time we got there, the bodies had started to stink, and so we took them out into a field south of town and burned them and their wagons and gave their horses to George. The five rebels that survived were put in jail. When the circuit judge came to town he held a trial, and then hung them. The year I turned thirty-seven, the hotel in town burnt down. The owner was leaving town, and so I found him and asked him if I could buy the burnt-out building. He laughed out loud, and said I could have it for a hundred dollars cash, and so I paid him. He signed the deed to the property over to me and laughed as he left town.

People in town thought I was mad, that is until I built a bigger hotel with a saloon on the side and called it The Sun Valley Hotel & Saloon and found good people to run them both. So now we owned the blacksmith shop, the hotel and saloon, a half interest in the mercantile store, three building lots in town, and two large pieces of land outside town. One evening we were having supper with Bob when he told us some of the town elders were talking about asking me to run for town council.if i said yes' he could put my name forward at the next council meeting. I told him I would think about it and let him know.

Jean and I went over to see George and Polly and told them what Bob had told us. We talked about it for a long time. George said it would be a good idea. Jean and Polly agreed, and so Jean and I went back and told Bob that

I would run for town council. He put my name forward to the elders, and I won a seat in the election. Everyone was pleased. I talked to Roy about running the valley while we lived in town. He said that with the good people he had, it would work out fine. So Jean and our kids moved with me to Hope. Now our children had other kids to play with, and Jean was happy. We lived with Bob, and life was good. We were seeing railroad surveyors east of town and knew they would be here soon. One afternoon, Frank came to town on a lumber wagon and found me in my office in the town hall.

He looked sad and had been crying, and so I asked him what was troubling him. He said his brother Boris had been fixing the drive-belt on his sawmill when his leg got caught in the belt driver. His leg got ripped off, and he died in minutes.

I put my arm around him and hugged him to me for a long time. Then we went to find Jean and told her what had happened to Boris. Jean started to cry and hugged Frank, and they both cried, and I felt a pain in my heart for them. So we took Frank out to the valley and buried Boris in our growing cemetery beside Angel and john Brown. We stayed there for two days Before we left, I put Frank in charge of the new sawmill. I think it made him feel a little better. After two years as a councilor, I ran for mayor and came in second. While this was going on more surveyors came to Hope, and then we knew the railroad was here. Two months later our mayor had a heart attack and died, and so the council asked me to take over as mayor.

By now the railroad was up to our town line, and would run alongside Hope, and on a property Jean and I owned. That made us very happy. One night at supper, Bob told us he was sick with a bad heart and would like to retire from the bank. He asked Jean to take over the bank. She said she would, and so Bob spent the rest of his life spoiling our children. They would make him laugh all the time. When he died, they cried all the way out to the valley. We buried him there in our cemetery.

•———○○○———•

That summer we built a school house in Hope and hired a teacher from Dallas, Texas. That fall the school opened with ten children and four adults. Jean was there to open the school and help the teacher settle in. The next week four more children and two more adults came and the school was full. Our town was growing. As mayor it was a good time, because everyone on council had ideas on how to expand the town. Some of the ideas were good. Some were really bad. And we made laws and regulations to govern the town when the railroad finally came into town.

Chapter 17

The Railroad

WE WERE NOW DIGGING DEEP IN THE GROUND AND FINDING lots of gemstones and small pockets of gold. Ezekiel was doing a good job of running the mine. One day, a gang of bandits came over the mountains and attacked the mine. There was seven of them. They shot and killed two miners and wounded Ezekiel in the leg, but he managed to get away and went for help. The bandits were setting dynamite to blow up the mine when something went wrong and the dynamite went off, killing six of the bandits. We found the seventh bandit wandering down the trail to the barn. He could not see out of his left eye and had cuts all over his body. Roy locked him in the barn, then went with Ezekiel to see what the explosion was all about and found the bandits all dead along with our two miners they had killed.

The explosion had caved in the entrance to the mine. Ezekiel said there were eight men in the mine, and so Roy went and told John to bring his men up to the mine. It took them five hours to dig their way into the mine. They found one dead miner, and the rest alive with broken bones and bad cuts, but they would make it. Roy sent a note with a lumber wagon that I was needed, and so I rode out to the valley and helped bury the dead and took the surviving bandit to town and the circuit judge held a trial, and then hung him.

One day the sheriff came to our council meeting asking for two more deputies and a larger jail and a bylaw to keep guns out of town. We voted in favour of the requests from the sheriff, and I had the clerk make up signs to say: *No Guns in Town*. All guns were to be left at the sheriff's office and would be returned on leaving town. We had the signs put up all over on buildings and posts.

That winter, the railroad engineers came to town to find a good place to set up their work camp, and so I showed them a piece of property I owned just outside of town. They said it would be a good place for their camp. A rental price was agreed to, and I told them I could supply all their food needs at the mercantile store, and so we went to see Sol. He gave them a good deal, and so they signed a contract with him, and he was very happy. Then they wanted to see my lumber mill, and so I took them out to our valley. They liked what they saw and gave me a one- year contract to supply railroad ties and lumber and stayed overnight and left in the morning. I told John about the order. He said he would start cutting ties with the new sawmill and lumber with the old one. He told me he had to use the two men I had planting new trees at the sawmills, and so I told him I would find two young lads to do the planting. I also told him to start shipping rail ties as soon as he could.

When I got back to town I put up a notice that I needed help at our sawmill. In the morning a small group of men were waiting for me when I got to my office. I spent the morning talking to them and hired two men, a woman cook, and two young lads to plant trees, and then sent them out to the valley on a lumber wagon with a note to Roy. For the next three weeks everyone worked very hard. Then the railroad gangs came to Hope and set up their camp and with them came gamblers, wild women, thieves, and all kinds of dubious people. We had to build a second hotel and a large saloon. A man came from Dallas, Texas and built a mercantile store at the other end of town. Then a dance hall went up and two more saloons. Now you could hear music all night.

In a very short time our town grew ten times its original size. Large groups of people crowded the sidewalks, and at least one person a week would be run over by a wagon and killed. The jail was always full. As mayor I sat in court each morning handing out fines to the sorry-looking men and the odd woman. Each night there would be at least two knife fights and the odd hidden gun. The sheriff now had five deputies and two jailers. As fast as we could make laws the ner-do-wells would find a way around them. It was six months before the railroad people left. It was a wild time. Hope would never be the same again. The railroad bought one of my properties outside town to build the station on, and I was there the day they put up the sign on the building, saying: *Welcome to Hope New Mexico.* And I felt so proud.

After two years as mayor I resigned to spend more time running the small empire Jean and I had made, and so we moved back to the valley. That Christmas we hosted a dinner for everyone who worked for us. Tom and Sol came from town. It was held in a new meeting hall we had built to replace our old smaller one. Jean and the ladies cooked a great meal. The children decorated the hall. And Frank found the prefect Christmas tree. After turkey and lots of cold root beer, I called each employee up to receive a bonus. They had worked so hard. When it came to Frank's turn I said, "And here is the new general manager of Sun Valley, Frank Skrens." He did not move until John, who was sitting beside him, poked him in the ribs and told him he was being called. His face broke into a smile as he got up and shook my hand. I said, loud enough for everyone in the hall to hear, that he was now the general manager of Sun Valley and he had earned it.

Then I turned to Roy and handed him a large envelope. He did not know what was going on, because I had just given his job to Frank. He opened the envelope and took out some papers and started to read them. Then a shocked look came over his face. He gave the papers to Holly, who studied the papers for a few minutes, and then started to cry. Roy put his arms around her and looked at us and said, "Why me?"

Jean smiled at them and said that they had earned it. Holly finally stopped crying and asked me what it meant, and so I told her it was the title to half of Sun Valley and everything in it. I told Roy he had been with me from the start and had looked after the ranch while we lived in town and had earned it, and I loved him like a brother. He said he did not know what was going on when I gave his job to Frank. I laughed and told him he had a funny look on his face when I gave his job away. He punched me on my arm then, and gave me a big hug, and then he hugged Jean and kissed her.

Chapter 18

Our Town

THE YEAR I TURNED FORTY-EIGHT, OUR SON TANNER FIN-
ished law school and passed his bar exams and so became
a lawyer. Jean and I went to Chicago to see him graduate.
We gave him my family farm in Hebron as a present. With
our blessings, he sold it and built an office building on a
lot we owned in Hope. He started his law practice and
rented part of his building to a man who wanted to start a
newspaper, and so *The Hope Express* was born.

Our second son went to college in Dallas, Texas and
studied cattle breeding. When he finished school we gave
him a thousand acres of grassland at the bottom of the
valley to raise cattle. Our daughter Emery went to finishing
school in New York and came home with a young man she
was madly in love with who had just finished law school,
and so Tanner put him to work in his law office and Emery
went to work in the bank. Three months later they got
married and had a big wedding. We gave them Bob's house

as a wedding gift. Roy and Holly's two girls went to school in Dallas, Texas and stayed there. Roy and Holly went to see them twice a year. Frank married a miner's daughter and built a house next to Ezekiel's house. Ezekiel's sister-in-law Dedria married a man who worked at the sawmill, and they built their house next to Frank's. One day I stopped and looked around our valley and thought to myself that we were truly building our own town.

And then one morning Frank came to our house and told me he had a big problem at the mine. He said two of the new miners got drunk on home-made spirits and killed the cook, and then killed each other.

I sent for the sheriff. He said it was a sad affair, and the miners got what they deserved, and so we buried them in our growing cemetery. I sent to town for two more miners and a cook. A month later one of our new miners put too much powder in a drill hole. The blast collapsed part of the mineshaft. While they were cleaning out the shaft one of the miners found a chunk of rock with a vein of gold running through it. Ezekiel brought it to the house and told me they found it when they were cleaning out the shaft, and so I went with him up to the mine and he showed me where they had found it. We looked for an hour and could not find where it had fallen from, and then the one of the miners wiped the dust off the side wall, and there it was: a large vein of gold running along the side of the shaft. We had been digging beside it for at least twenty feet and had not realized it, even though it was so close.

o———oOo———o

At our weekly meeting Ezekiel had a miner with him. This miner told us he had worked at a mine that used steam drilling machines that made the work faster than a hammer and chisel, and that they also had a rock crusher that made it easier to get the gold out.

By now we had a telegraph line out to the valley, and so I sent a telegraph message to my supplier and ordered a drill rig and a rock crusher and a big steam plant. While we waited for the drilling equipment—which the supplier said would be here in about three weeks—we built a building for the steam plant and a new cookhouse and an addition to the bunkhouse. Our old sawmill was getting slow, and so we only cut timbers for the mine, and now that our contract with the railroad had run out we went back to cutting lumber full time. With the railroad we could ship lumber to other towns, and we could never keep up with the orders coming in. When the drilling equipment arrived it had two men with it to show us how to set it up and how to use it. They ended up staying. By now we had more than fifty men and twenty women working on our ranch and ten children of school age and it was a busy place, and so Jean said she would like to build a school house and a store. I thought it was a grand idea. So we built them as well as a new, larger meeting hall.

—○——○○○——○—

The year I turned fifty we invited everyone in the valley and all the families living off the valley to a Thanksgiving dinner and dance with us in our new meeting hall. Jean and Holly along with the women in our valley cooked the dinner and Frank was put in charge of getting enough tables and chairs, and I hired a group of musicians to play at the dance. Roy and Holly's two daughters came, and they brought their husbands from Dallas. A special invitation also went out to George and Polly and Sol and our blacksmith Tom. We had over seventy people sit down to dinner. As I sat there and looked out over the crowd of smiling faces I thought how I was once a beaten twelve-year-old boy running from parents, and then young man working on a wagon train. I thought of all the adventures I had in between, and then how I found all this. It made a tear come to my eyes.

Jean looked at me and asked me what was wrong.

"I'm happy." She touched my arm and smiled. At the dance, two of Sanders' cowboys got into a fight over a pretty young lady and gave each other a black eye, and the young lady went home alone, and we all had a good time.

Two days after Thanksgiving a young couple came up to the house in a covered wagon. I went out to meet them. The young man got down and said his name Adam. I told him my name and shook his hand, and then he looked at the woman in the wagon and said she was his wife, Alice, and he said George at the livery stable in Hope had told him he might find work out here. I smiled at them and thought to myself 'I will have to talk to George about sending anymore strays out to our valley.' I asked them to come up onto the porch and have a seat. Alice turned and picked up a small girl and helped her down. Adam told me she was their daughter Mary, and so I called to Jean to come and meet them, and could she bring some cold root beer with her. Mary liked the root beer and asked for more, and we laughed.

I told Jean that George had sent them, and she smiled at me. Jean asked them where they had come from. Adam said they had come all the way from Crofordville, Georgia looking for a good place to bring up a family. We talked with them for a while, and then Jean asked Adam if he would like to run the store we had just built. He told us he would like that, and Alice told us she had gone to school to be a book keeper, and so Jean put her to work in our company office. The bunk house beside the barn was not being used, and so I told them to move in there for now. They thanked me and went to move in. One night after supper, Jean and I were sitting on our porch having coffee and looking out over our valley and wondering at all we had accomplished when Jean said she wished we could spend more time together, because life was going by so fast. I looked at her and asked what was on her mind. She looked back at me and said we had made a very large fortune and were not enjoying it. Then she said it would be nice to go on a long holiday. I smiled at her and said: "It never entered my mind that there was a life outside our valley."

Then I stood up and pulled her to me and hugged her, and said I was so sorry for being so selfish, and I would love to go on a long holiday with her. She hugged me back and kissed me and said she loved me so much.

○────○○○────○

So after two months of planning and lots of meetings, Roy took us to Hope and put us on a train to start a new adventure.

The End

www.ingramcontent.com/pod-product-compliance
Lightning Source LLC
Chambersburg PA
CBHW051807050726
47598CB00006B/2455